HEBERDEN'S SEAT

DOUGLAS CLARK

PERENNIAL LIBRARY

Harper & Row, Publishers

New York, Cambridge, Philadelphia, San Francisco
London, Mexico City, São Paulo, Singapore, Sydney

A hardcover edition of this book was published by Victor Gollancz Ltd. It is here reprinted by arrangement with the author.

HEBERDEN'S SEAT. Copyright © 1979 by Douglas Clark. All rights reserved. Printed in the United States of America. No part of this book may be used or reproduced in any manner whatsoever without written permission except in the case of brief quotations embodied in critical articles and reviews. For information address John Farquharson, Ltd., 250 West 57th Street, Room 410, New York, N.Y. 10107. Published simultaneously in Canada by Fitzhenry & Whiteside Limited, Toronto.

First PERENNIAL LIBRARY edition published 1984.

Library of Congress Cataloging in Publication Data

Clark, Douglas.
    Heberden's seat.

    Originally published: London: V. Gollancz, 1979.
    I. Title.
PR6053.L294H4   1984   823'.914   84-47664
ISBN 0-06-080724-5 (pbk.)

84   85   86   87   88   10   9   8   7   6   5   4   3   2   1

For Christopher and Andrew Sweeney

— 1 —

"Even I know," said Detective Chief Inspector Green, "that you don't switch off the engine and freewheel uphill. Downhill, perhaps, on occasion, although that is strictly illegal. So switch on again, lad, and carry on motoring."

The big police Rover was coasting even more slowly to a halt as the low rise took the way off it.

"I haven't switched off," replied Detective Sergeant Reed through clenched teeth. "The bastard's given up on me."

"Language," chided Green, who seemed to be in an amiable mood. "Our cars don't give up on us."

"This one has. There's no ignition. No electrics."

While he was speaking, Reed had drawn the car into the side of the narrow country road. There was no footpath, just a lush grass verge standing too high above the tarmac for the unpowered wheels to mount and, thereby, leave the way clear for passing traffic.

"Have a look at it," said Detective Superintendent Masters, opening the rear offside door and stepping out. "We'll stretch our legs for a bit."

It was a gorgeous afternoon in June. Masters and his team were returning from a week spent in helping the police in Middlesbrough to sort out a rather convoluted mess of theft, thuggery and murder. It would have been quicker to have taken the motorway south, but knowing Green's innate—and growing—fear of fast and cluttered roads, Masters had suggested that they should find a scenic route and take their time over reaching London. And this is how the four of them now came to be stranded on a small, deserted, country road twenty or so miles north of Lincoln.

Detective Sergeant Berger, who had been sitting alongside Reed in the front of the car, announced his intention of walking up to the top of the rise to see if there was a house close by should they need a phone to summon help. Reed lifted the bonnet and started to peer around inside.

"These tall hedges," said Green, lighting a cigarette from a crumpled Kensitas packet, "stop you seeing anything. We might as well be in the Colorado Canyon."

Masters, who was filling his pipe with Warlock Flake, looked about him. "If you want to look about, there's a gate in the hedge just ahead, and a convenient tree to climb."

Surprisingly, Green replied: "That's an idea. I haven't climbed a tree for years. When I was a lad, I used to go scrumping apples."

"Alternator connections," said Reed, raising his head. "The lead's off."

"Can you fix it?"

"I can put it back, Chief. But I think we've been going for heaven knows how long without recharging the battery. It's as flat as a pancake now. Not enough in it to spark the plugs."

"In other words you need help."

"A car with a set of jump leads to start me up would do it."

"Stay with it. The DCI and I will walk up to join Berger. He may have located a phone. If so, I'll call for a local Panda car."

Berger was on his way back. They met him just before the top of the rise.

"There's an old church here, Chief. Nothing else before the village in the next dip."

"How far?"

"Half a mile, about."

"Keep walking, son," said Green, turning Berger round

2

by the elbow. "The battery's flat. You sort that for us while the DS and I have a snooze in the churchyard."

Berger set off, his jacket slung over his shoulder, with a finger crooked in the hanger. Masters and Green followed more slowly. Masters would have preferred a faster pace—his long legs demanded it—but Green, heavier built and shorter, and wearing a heavy suit in rough, dark material, was beginning to sweat. The globules glistened on his forehead and on his upper lip. Two or three drops had started to cascade down from his temples to his heavy jowls by the time they reached the gate of the old church which Berger had mentioned.

It was on the left of the road. An old, grey oak, double gate planted in the hedgerow. Fastened to the left-hand leaf was a rectangular piece of hardboard on which was stuck a typewritten sheet.

"'Tombstone Notice,'" grunted Green, mopping his face with his handkerchief. "What's that when it's at home?"

"I'm as wise as you are," replied Masters, stooping to read the sun-faded lettering.

"What's it say?"

"In essence? That St John the Divine's church—presumably this one—was declared a redundant church some five years ago and is now under offer to a prospective buyer who intends to use the premises for non-ecclesiastical purposes. The buyer in question proposes to sink a cesspit in the churchyard and to clear the ground for use as a domestic garden. Parishioners are informed that should they wish to have the buried remains of any near relative transferred, as a result of this proposal, from this site to other consecrated ground, it can be arranged at the expense of the Church Commissioners. Only those who are close kindred of deceased buried here may apply, and the Commissioners are empowered to refuse free transfer for bodies buried more than ten years before the date of display of this notice. And that is, the 3rd of June this year."

"I'm not surprised it's redundant. It's in the middle of

nowhere. There aren't all that many faithful left these days, and those there are won't walk half a mile out of the village to get to church."

Masters opened the right-hand leaf, which was on the latch. They entered the churchyard slowly.

"It's sadly overgrown."

"You're telling me. Grass waist-high and all ready to seed. It's a wilderness. The bloke who's taking this on will need a flame thrower to clear it." Green led the way along the remnants of a path that led to the south door. It was just possible to see that the way had never been properly paved. Yellow gravel lay on top of mud hard-packed over the years by the feet of those attending services at the little church. Now the tall grasses on either side almost met above it and through it poked finer grass and weeds.

Green forged ahead towards the porch at the west door. He reached it and lifted the latch ring. "Locked," he said, sounding so disappointed that Masters began to wonder if Green had hidden religious leanings.

"Closed for five years. Except that whoever is about to buy it must have looked it over before he made his bid."

Green grunted. "Sunny end?" he asked nodding towards the near south-west corner. "Full in the sun round there."

He was right. The west end was full in the afternoon sun. Here, in front of the great west door, was a semi-circle of beaten earth not yet invaded by the approaching undergrowth. On this plot, dragged across the door as though to get the maximum benefit from the sun, was an old oak bench. It had weathered down to an ashen colour, and gave the impression that it was as old as the church itself. A small plaque screwed to the middle of the top slat at the back told them different. The bench had been given by one Alexander Heberden, as recently as 1961, to "provide a place of rest for those who would tarry awhile in the environs of the church."

"It's been used quite a lot recently," said Green. "The

seat's not mucky. It looks as if it's been polished by quite a few backsides recently. Courting couples, I suppose."

Masters made no comment. He turned to face the sun and lifted his hand to shade his eyes. "It'll be too uncomfortable to sit here, unless we move the seat."

"Let's walk round," said Green.

They went in single file, clockwise round the church. As they approached the eastern end of the north side, Green said: "Another door."

"Vestry, perhaps."

It was a small, narrow door, with two stone steps up to it and a pointed arch at the top.

"Solid oak, again," said Green. "And it has been used pretty often. You can see the grease marks round the keyhole."

"What have we here?" Masters had moved a step or two from the church into the waist-high grass. "A well?"

Green joined him. "That's right. There wouldn't be water laid on in a church this far out. But they'd need it for cleaning and filling the flower vases at festival times."

"Dangerous," said Masters. "The surround is only two feet high."

"If you'd ever had to draw water from a well you'd know that getting it up's hard enough without having a wall six feet high. There's no windlass, you know. You just drop a bucket on the end of a rope."

"Still, I'd like to see it covered over."

"It probably was—by boards. They'll have gone, unless they're somewhere in the long grass."

Masters peered into the well. He looked for a few seconds and then turned round to search the ground. He saw what he wanted near the vestry door. Some of the yellow stones were still to be seen. He went across and selected three of the biggest.

"Dropping stones down wells?" asked Green, with a slight sneer. "I thought you'd be over the kid stuff."

"Just listen," said Masters.

"To see how deep it is?"

5

"Listen." Masters' tone was mandatory.

The first stone went down. Both waited for it to strike water.

"Anything?" asked Masters.

Green shook his head. "It's dry. It probably dries out in summer."

"I thought I saw the shimmer of water."

"Drop another stone."

Again they waited for a splash that didn't come.

Green leaned over the parapet. The well was barely a yard in diameter and the sun did not penetrate its depth. With a grunt of annoyance, after squinting hard down the shaft, Green took out his matches. He struck one and held it down at arm's length.

"There's water," he said, straightening up. "I could just see the sheen."

"Anything else?"

Masters' tone caused Green to peer at him. "Like what?"

"I'll drop another stone."

Again no splash.

"Come on," said Green. "What do you reckon is down there?"

"Clothes," said Masters. "A white shirt, I think."

"Clothes? Wait a minute. You caught a glimpse of something down there?"

Masters nodded.

"Well it isn't a shirt," said Green adamantly. "If it was and it was floating just at the surface, a stone would still splash. But if the stone were to hit a floating body...." Green didn't finish. He again leaned over the parapet and struck three matches at once to give him more light. When he straightened up he said: "I can't be sure. I thought I saw something white. But it could have been because you suggested it."

Masters nodded. "But we've got to make sure. Stay here. I'll get the torches from the car."

Without Green to slow him down, Masters made good time. He returned with a torch and a ball of thin twine from the murder bag. He handed them to Green. "You lower, while I look."

Three minutes later, Green said: "It's a man. A fully grown man. He's come to the top, but there isn't enough room for him to float horizontally, so his body is jammed in a sort of curve."

"You can pull the light up now."

"And then do what?"

"Wait. I told Reed that when Berger got back he was to send him here to us, together with a local bobby if he's got one in tow."

The local bobby was Sergeant Iliff. It was obvious from his demeanour that Berger had briefed him fully as to the identity of the visitors from Scotland Yard. He listened dutifully while Masters told him of the discovery of the body and then, very sensibly, asked if he could borrow the torch and the string to make his own inspection.

"How're you going to get him up then, lad?" asked Green. "There's not much room for a man to work down there."

Iliff considered the problem for a moment.

"Grappling hooks."

"No good," said Masters. "You'd be able to hook into his clothes easily enough, but he won't come up in his present posture. He'd jam across the shaft. You'll have to extract him either head first or feet first."

"I'll send for the gear, sir," replied Iliff, obviously unwilling to stay and exchange ideas about the retrieval of the corpse. "Could I ask you, sir, to call in and see DCI Webb at the Market Rasen station? He'd best hear it from you himself, sir."

"You want us to go off our route for a suicide?" asked Green. "We're on our way home after a tiring job, sergeant."

"Even so, sir," replied Iliff courteously. "We like official statements from whoever finds bodies in this Division.

7

How they came to discover the corpse and so on. And you must agree it sounds a bit odd for two senior officers from Scotland Yard to happen on a dead body in a well that nobody can see down in a disused churchyard in the middle of nowhere."

Masters glanced across at Green. "I do believe we're being regarded as suspects."

"Nobody's above the law, sir," said Iliff. "I'll send a message to the DCI to expect you. Your car will likely be started by now. We brought leads with us to start you up from our battery. PC Bannerman will have sorted it for you."

Masters had difficulty not smiling in the face of Iliff's correctness. But he agreed amicably enough to do as he had been asked, and led the way from the well back to the churchyard gate, taking great care to go round the church itself in a clockwise direction.

DCI Webb was inclined to laugh when Masters said he had been ordered to report. But the local man's mirth was not long-lasting nor, or so it seemed to Masters, very happy.

"You're worried," said Masters. "This body in a well is causing you some concern. You've been expecting it, or looking for it. Am I right?"

"Sit down, sir, please," begged Webb. "All of you gentlemen. I'll have some tea sent in."

"Now you're talking," said Green, drawing a chair up to Webb's desk. "On a hot afternoon like this, a mug of chai is just what I need to cool me down."

The others settled down while Webb phoned for tea, then Masters said: "Seeing we shall be here for a few minutes, why not tell us all about it? The telling itself might help and who knows? One of us might have a useful idea."

Webb nodded. He was a thickset man of forty, but his hair was still jet-black and, cut short at the sides, was brushed back flat on top. He was red-faced and already needed another shave. His eyes were those of a pleasant man slightly bewildered and troubled.

"Out with it then," urged Green. "It's not as if you can have anything horrific to tell us about a nice part of the country like this."

"At any other time," said Webb, "I'd have agreed with you, Mr Green. But would you believe that in the middle of all this I've got two mysterious disappearances and a fire-bug who's started five fires? In this weather, when everything's tinder dry?"

Masters ignored the reference to a fire-raiser, although he was aware that in farming country such people are probably regarded as greater menaces than their counterparts in towns. "Disappearances? Who?"

"Both grown men in their forties."

"And when we said we thought the body in the well was that of a grown man, you thought one of your missing two had probably come to light?"

Webb nodded.

"So what?" asked Green. "Now you've only got one missing."

"Have I? The two men were great friends. And I don't mean anything other than what I say. Mates, that's all. One had a legal wife, the other a common-law wife. But they were real mates."

"I see. So now you think that as one has turned up in a well, the other will show up dead, too?"

"Either that or—"

"Or they had a barney as close mates have been known to have," said Green, "and that one has killed his pal and, after disposing of the body, has scarpered."

"It could be what has happened."

"Too true. So you'd have a murder case on your hands. Unless the other one turns up dead, too. In which case you may have a double murder to cope with."

"Right. I've been thinking about it ever since Sergeant Iliff told me about the body in the well. I don't reckon two men would make a suicide pact, do you? So I may be faced with looking for a third party who did for them both."

While everybody was pondering this in silence, a constable entered with a tray. "No biscuits, sir," he whispered hoarsely in Webb's ear, "so I've brought five slabs of grit cake."

"Thanks."

As the constable left the office, Masters said: "I think much will depend on the pathologist's report."

"I've arranged for it to be done immediately. If they get the body up in time it'll be done this evening."

"Good. Now you say these two men disappeared. Did they disappear simultaneously?"

Webb gestured a request to Berger to pour the tea while he continued his conversation with Masters.

"That's the mystery, sir. They didn't. Ten days apart, in fact."

"Ah," said Green, striving to remove the plastic wrapping from round his slab of grit cake. "Sinister. Or could be. If the bloke in the well is one of them, which was he? The one who went missing first? Or second?" He used his teeth to tear the wrapping. "It'll make a difference."

"In what way?" asked Reed.

"Let's dispose of the coincidence business first," interrupted Masters. "Because there is a thumping great coincidence here, pointed by the fact that the two men disappeared at different times. Had they both dropped out simultaneously, it would have been easy to suppose that they had both met with a fatal accident while in each other's company, or had agreed to push off together to South America without informing their wives. But for two men to disappear, in the same area, within a few days of each other, with the added factor that they are inseparable friends, argues that lightning has struck in the same place twice. And that isn't on.

"So if it is a coincidence, it's a man-made one. As DCI Green says, if the body in the well is that of one of the two missing men, it will make a difference if it is number one or number two. If it is number one, it could be that number two killed him and then, after a lapse of time, disappeared. If it is number two, where is number one?"

"Number two could have committed suicide in a fit of

remorse at killing number one."

"Of course he could. But I venture to suggest that in such a case, the one who committed suicide would leave a note telling us where he had hidden the other's body. As Mr Webb has said he has no knowledge of what has happened to the two men, it means no note has been left."

"That's right," agreed Webb. He picked up the phone on his desk as it started to ring. The others busied themselves with their tea and cake as he spoke.

"Mrs Heberden, did you say? She's been away for a week and returned to find...no sign of her husband? He's been away three or four days? How does she know? Mail, papers and milk. I see. Right, Sergeant, I'll look into it. Ring Mrs Heberden and tell her I'll be out there as soon as I can."

He put the phone down and looked across at Masters. "There's been another one, sir."

"Disappearance?"

"Alexander Heberden. He's a fairly wealthy landowner. In his sixties...."

"Wealthy?" asked Green, disbelievingly. "And the milk was left on the doorstep?"

Webb shrugged. "He and his wife live at the Grange. It's big, too big, for them. But they have the help of a married couple living in and a charwoman for the heavy work. The garden is done on contract. One of these firms with three or four men in a lorry descends once a fortnight to trim the edges and hoe the beds. Every summer about now they close the house, more or less."

"You mean they send their couple away on holiday?"

"That's it. But they don't necessarily go off themselves or together."

"Coincidentally, you mean?"

Webb nodded. "Mrs Heberden usually goes off on one of these artistic package holidays. She goes off and dabbles with about fifty others who all live in some hotel where they're supposed to get instruction in drawing and so on."

"I know the sort of thing."

11

"Yes. Well, the old man doesn't go. He's quite a busy sort of man. He manages his own properties, you see, so he's always going and coming."

"So it is conceivable that he remained behind alone in the house?"

"From what I heard on the phone, he was to be there for just two nights alone and then he was going off to some big agricultural show down in the west country. He was to judge some classes, I believe. I suppose he was instructed by his wife to cancel the milk and papers but apparently never got round to it."

Masters shrugged. "He could have forgotten. Your best plan is to ring the secretary of the show he was supposed to attend. He could be there, or could have been there."

"Mrs Heberden did that as soon as she got back home. The secretary of the show said Heberden hadn't turned up. He'd rung through to the Grange several times to try to get hold of Heberden, but without any luck."

Berger said: "You've got an epidemic, Mr Webb. Two epidemics. One of missing persons and one of mysterious fires."

Webb nodded. "I'll have to go now, to see Mrs Heberden. I don't suppose...?"

"What?" asked Masters.

Webb looked slightly sheepish. "Well, sir, you gentlemen are always available to help should any other force need help. And I need help. Definitely."

Masters glanced across at Green who was carefully withdrawing a Kensitas with the nail of thumb and forefinger and who—or so it seemed—refused to meet his gaze. Masters knew the problem. Green had been away for some days and now wanted to get back home. But he was too good a copper to want to refuse help where it was needed. The DCI was, at the moment, unable to solve his personal equation and was waiting to hear how Masters tackled the problem.

Seeing he was to get no help, Masters had no option but to say to Webb: "It will have to be done officially.

Your Chief Constable will have to make a formal request to the Assistant Commissioner, Crime. And don't forget that your senior officers may not want us, even though you do."

"Will you stay until I can sort it out?"

"I think your best plan would be to ask your headquarters to request that we should stay, without prejudice, until you have the forensic report on the body in the well. If you could hurry that along, so that you have at least a preliminary report by, say eight o'clock, that outcome might decide whether we stay over tonight or not."

The call came from the pathologist at twenty past seven. He was willing to give them a preliminary report if they would care to motor the sixteen miles to Lincoln in order to hear it.

Curiously enough, the time which had elapsed since Webb left them about five o'clock had been spent, not in discussing whatever case might eventuate, but in wandering round Market Rasen, noting its racecourse, its old De Aston Grammar School, cattlemarket, church and, almost inevitably, in sampling the beer in The Chestnut Tree, the largest of the local hostelries. Reed had arranged for his battery to be given a crash charge, and it was he who brought the message to Masters that a forensic report was ready. Masters, in the middle of giving the barman an order, cancelled it and asked his colleagues to join the car.

"Is Webb coming?" asked Green.

"He set off as soon as he'd found me and given me a message for the Chief."

"We'll get there, will we?"

"The battery's been given a charge. I know it's damaging to force it. I'd always prefer to trickle charge, but needs must when the devil drives."

"See there's no devil driving this tank," grunted Green, who was highly nervous in cars and so always selected what he considered to be the safest seat—the nearside rear. "Take your time getting there and remember everybody else on the road is a fool."

Despite Green's instructions, they arrived at the forensic laboratory a minute or so before eight, and were met by Webb and Dr Watling, the pathologist.

"Masters?" said Watling. "I've heard of you. Several times as a matter of fact. There aren't too many chaps like me about, so the few of us who do exist tend to chatter among ourselves like washer-women in a public laundry. You've often been the subject of our conversation."

"I'm flattered, Dr Watling. Is what *you've* got for us likely to get me talked about?"

Watling, in slacks and shirt sleeves, picked up his notes from the desk. "It depends on what you make of it, but I think yes. You see, dead men don't throw themselves down wells."

Green asked: "He didn't drown?"

"No. Dead on arrival in the well. No water at all in the lungs and tubes."

"How was he killed?"

"That's a question I can't answer directly. All I can give is the general verdict that he died from respiratory depression so severe as to be fatal."

"Meaning what? He stopped breathing?"

Watling laughed. "You could say that, Mr Green, because that is precisely what happened. But what I mean is he wasn't injured in any way—shot, knifed, coshed or strangled—to cause death. The respiratory depression caused him to stop breathing and so to die, but what caused the respiratory depression is another matter."

"Heart attack of one sort or another?" asked Masters.

Watling shook his head. "Heart as sound as a bell. No signs of thrombi or other obstructions—"

"Obstructions?" broke in Green. "Something in his throat that blocked the air intake?"

"Throat clear, I'm afraid."

"So where do we stand?" asked Masters.

Watling paused before replying. "I have been over the

14

body very carefully. It has been in water for four or five days, I'd say, so there's a lot of swelling and a sort of blotting-paper effect with epidermis, so it is possible I have missed some minute hypodermic puncture. But I think not. Nor can I see any signs of ingestion of toxic substance—no burning of the lips or oesophagus or anything of that sort."

"Discolouration of the organs?"

"Not so far."

"A puzzle."

"It means I have to do some extremely careful analysis, because I can think of no way in which a healthy man could suffer a lethal bout of respiratory depression unless that depression was caused by a foreign substance."

"Foreign substance?" asked Berger.

"Everything that goes into the body is foreign. Even food and drink. But I was thinking of chemicals and medicines mostly. Quite a number of drugs have respiratory depression as a side effect. Rarely fatally so, of course, but heroin, for example, causes it in a dose-related way."

"So you think he was poisoned?"

"If you care to put it that way, yes. I also think he was murdered, because, as I said, corpses don't throw themselves down wells."

Masters nodded and turned to Webb. "Has the body been identified?"

"Not identified as yet, sir, but recognised. It's number two."

"The second of the two friends to disappear?"

"The same. Name of Rex Belton, the local representative of a farm machinery firm."

"I said it would be sinister," commented Green. "One goes missing and a few days later his pal is murdered. No suicide in a fit of remorse. Murder. Probably two murders—if the first one's body shows up."

Webb said, glumly: "And Alexander Heberden gone, too. It might mean we've got a maniac loose."

"I take it," said Masters, "that your headquarters would

now definitely like us to take over?"

"That was the agreement with the Yard, sir. If murder was established, we could call on your services."

"In that case, we've a job of work to do." He turned to Watling. "When can I expect your full report, doctor?"

"Tomorrow at this time?"

"Fine. I'll ring you. So if you'll excuse us now, my team and I have a few things to do, not least among which is to find somewhere to lay our heads."

"Don't worry about that," said Webb. "I took the precaution of making provisional bookings at the Chestnut Tree."

They had a late dinner. The staff at The Chestnut Tree weren't too pleased about it, but Webb seemed to have the resources and enough local authority to make it possible. Consequently he joined them at table, and his presence gave Masters his first opportunity as officer in charge of the investigation to ask the questions to which he wanted answers.

As he dissected a grilled sole, he said: "We know two names. Rex Belton, who is the gentleman down the well, and Alexander Heberden, who is one of those missing. Who is the third man?"

"John Melada."

"Sounds foreign."

"He's British. There may have been a bit of Latin blood there somewhere—Italian or Spanish—but if so, I know nothing of it."

Reed raised a hand with a fork in it. "Can I butt in, Chief?"

"Go ahead."

"You seem to be linking all these cases. I know Mr Webb links Belton with Melada and the reasons for that are obvious. But why assume Heberden is connected with those two in any way? Did they all three live close together? Were they friends?"

Masters turned to Webb for the answers to the last two parts of Reed's multiple question.

"Melada and Belton live just outside Lincoln. Not in the city itself, otherwise they wouldn't be in the County Divisional area. It's about twelve or fourteen miles to where they live. But Heberden lives not far from the church where you found Belton. Actually, he owns a deal of land between the two villages of Oakby and Beckby. In fact the parish is called Oakby-cum-Beckby. But as far as I know, Heberden was not friendly with the other two. I mean, it's not likely, is it?"

"Why not?" growled Green. "You think because Heberden was the squire the other two wouldn't be in his class?"

Webb seemed surprised by Green's words and by the tone of his voice, but he answered readily enough. "If that's how you want to put it, that's exactly what I think. But there are other factors. First, Heberden was much older than the other two, so the generation gap would keep them apart. Second, they lived miles away from each other, so it's not likely they knew each other casually."

Reed came in again. "That's what I thought, and it's why I asked the Chief if he was linking the three cases."

Green, still a bit grumpy because his socialist principles had been outraged, said: "They're all missing, aren't they? Doesn't that link them?"

Before Reed could reply, Masters said: "Quite right. But there's more than that."

"Oh yes?"

"Belton disappeared down a well in the yard of St John the Divine church in Oakby. Also in the churchyard of St John the Divine is an oak seat bearing a plaque with the donor's name. That name is Alexander Heberden—I read it this afternoon."

Webb laid down his knife and fork and stared at Masters in amazement. "You're sure?"

"If the chief says so," grunted Berger, "he's sure."

"Less concrete, but still a strong possibility—as a link between Belton and Heberden—is the fact that Belton is a representative for a firm selling agricultural machinery, and Heberden is a land-owner on Belton's patch. If Belton was any use as a salesman he would have made sure he called on everybody in the area who might use the implements he sold and—or so I think—he would make sure that he knew potential customers and that they knew him."

"Heberden doesn't actually farm himself," said Webb.

"So what?" asked Green. "If he has tenant farmers his influence could be just what a rep would try to get. Heberden could recommend his tenants to buy certain items which Belton had to sell. In fact, it would pay Belton to cultivate Heberden, if you'll pardon the pun."

"Christmas night!" said Webb. "I hadn't thought of that."

"Perhaps you could establish that they were acquainted," said Masters to the local man. "It may help us if we know for sure."

Webb nodded. Reed asked: "And the fires? Are they linked, too, Chief?"

Masters carefully turned the half skeleton of his grilled sole before replying. Having thus exposed the white underbelly, he paused before dissecting it. "At the moment I confess I can think of no reason to suppose that they are. However, Mr Webb says they are unusual—in that such spates of fire-raising are infrequent in his area. That alone should not be a cause for regarding them as significant in the case of the murdered Belton simply because it, too, is unusual for the same reason. Nor, however, is it a cause for disregarding them entirely." He carefully parted a portion of fish down one of the longitudinal striations. "But if we are not to disregard them, then we must pay them some attention. So far, we know nothing of them, except that they are five in number—two hayricks, two old barns, and a veterinary surgeon's premises. I can surmise nothing from that information. But we shall see when we know more."

"That's as good a way of saying nothing as I've come across in a month of Sundays," said Green, wiping his mouth on his napkin. "Any more spuds on that dish in front of you, young Berger? If not, flag-wag for some more."

"Is it?" asked Masters, sensing an old belligerence in Green's tones. "If I have said nothing in reply to Reed's last question, perhaps you will supply the answer."

Green replied without thought: "You can't link the fires to the murders. There's no evidence to say you should."

"Go on."

"So why waste time on them?"

"You're saying we should ignore them."

Green stared hard at Masters. "No you don't."

"Don't what?"

"Catch me that way. Once you have mentioned it as being possibly connected, even in the slightest way with Belton's murder, and it turns out that he's as much as motored past the sites of one of those fires, even if it was ten years ago last muck-spreading, you'll crow like an old hen."

"So?"

"We'll look into them, with the excuse that it's best to do so even if only to eliminate them from the investigation."

The waiter, somewhat ungraciously, plonked a metal serving dish of freshly fried chips in front of Green who, from that point on, appeared to lose all interest in the discussion, preferring to concentrate on his food.

Webb asked: "How are you going to start, sir?"

Masters took his time in replying. "You probably think we've been having a bit of a slanging match so far. But I assure you, all that we have really been doing is clearing our minds. However, to answer your question more directly, I propose to start with people. Belton had a wife. He also had a friend, Melada, who, though he has apparently disappeared, had a common-law wife. And there's Mrs Heberden. So there are three to start with. They may lead us to others. Then there are places. The church for instance, and the sites of the fires. By the time we've got so far, we should be able to get to events about which we so far know nothing."

"Do you always work like that?"

"No. We treat each case on its merits; and don't try to hold me to any timetable or sequence. We have to maintain flexibility of approach." Masters put his knife and fork together on the plate. "Of course, we ought to have a better idea of how to proceed once we get the forensic report."

"Ought to have?"

"Your pathologist didn't seem too sure that he would be able to give us much help."

"Oh, he will. Watling's a sound man."

Masters laughed. "You do realise what you've just said, don't you?"

Webb looked bewildered.

"If Watling is so sound, why shouldn't I believe his preliminary report? A good pathologist who admits to being unable to find a hypodermic mark is probably correct right at the start."

"I see what you mean. If he's good, his first report is right, so you won't expect much more from him."

"It's a logical conclusion. I have to keep it in mind. Let's hope I'm wrong."

"Thereby proving me wrong about Watling."

Masters grinned. "There's a lot to do. Don't let's start by assuming we're wrong about anything."

Green finished his course and pushed the plate away. "That's better! Now, where are we? Lemon meringue pie for pud? Fair do's. I'll have a double helping."

Webb stared at him, hard. Green noticed the look.

"What's up, lad? Wondering why I want a double helping? It's because I've got two men's work to do, son."

"Meaning mine and your own?"

"You said it."

Webb turned to Masters. "Just as a matter of interest, sir, what can I do to help?"

"Provide us with a second car. I'd like you to help Mr Green and Sergeant Berger tomorrow morning. He'll be eliminating the fires, and as you know the district you'll be invaluable to him."

"What about a guide for you?"

"Perhaps your Sergeant Iliff...."

"Uniform branch? Look, sir. The fires were on Iliff's patch, so he could escort Mr Green...."

"Suits me," said Green. "I took a shine to that boyo. He as good as told His Nibs here he was under suspicion for murder. I liked that."

— 2 —

"Where to, Chief?" asked Reed at half past eight the next morning.

"Follow Mr Webb's instructions. I want to go to the Belton house, but I think we're a little too early for that. A woman who learned only last night that she is a widow won't welcome visitors before the streets are aired, so we'll have a look at the church first."

As they motored, Masters questioned Webb as to what steps he had taken at St John the Divine's after the body had been found.

"None, really. The big thing was to get the body up and away. After that I told Iliff to keep a man at the site. I expected you to be involved so I gave instructions that the constable on duty was to stay near the gate and not to trample near the well in case you wanted to examine the ground."

"Thanks. I did look about me while I was there yesterday, and so did Green. I know the grass is long, but I don't think there's anything there for us."

The roads were not too busy, and Reed made good time. It was another glorious day, with the clearness of air only to be found in countryside unpolluted by industry. The hedgerows were burdened with foliage and wild roses—single, frail, pale pink blossom—and the trees stood motionless, untroubled by any breeze across the flat landscape. It was only as they approached Oakby that there was any really noticeable rise and fall of hill and valley.

"What are we approaching?" asked Masters. "The Lin-

colnshire Wolds or the Lincoln Edge? I can never remember which is further east."

"The Edge," replied Webb. "You can always tell. The
edge is limestone and broken in straight lines. The Wolds
are chalk and all gently rounded. You need to go up to
Louth and that area to see the Wolds properly. That's how
I tell."

"It doesn't look very broken," said Reed.

"Not just here, sergeant. It's just the odd rise about
here. The scarp itself is further over."

Less than half a mile after they left the village, climbing
gently as they went, they reached the church. The constable on duty had already removed his jacket, which now
hung on a gate post.

"Any trouble, constable?"

"No, sir, nothing. I relieved PC Arthur at six and there's
hardly a soul been past since I took over. He reported all
quiet during the night, too, sir."

Webb turned to Masters. "How long are you likely to
be here, Chief?"

Masters noted the form of address, which usually only
his own sergeants used, but did not remark on it.

"You'd like the constable to have a cup of tea, is that
it? Right. Send him off to the village. Say half an hour.
Reed can run him in."

"I've got my bike, sir," said the grateful constable. "Just
inside the hedge."

"Right. Cut along."

As the PC was retrieving his machine, Masters asked:
"Do you live in Oakby?"

"Yes, sir. I'm in Oakby. PC Arthur in Beckby."

Masters nodded and went through the gate. It was rather
difficult for him to get a true picture of the plot, because
it appeared to be entirely surrounded by trees and tall
hedges and to contain overgrown bushes and trees which
blocked the view. But it lay on the shallow hillside and
was, as far as he could make out, roughly square, with the
little church more or less in the middle. He made an

estimate of its size. Something over a hundred yards each way. His maths was still good enough to tell him that there would be approximately two acres of graves and tombstones all overgrown by a wilderness that hadn't been tended in any way for a number of years and, probably, only spasmodically for long enough before that.

The grass grew waist-high: rye grass all ready to seed and bring on yet more of its kind. Privet, yellow-spotted laurel, yew and even overgrown ribes. Self-set, they burgeoned between the graves that were scarcely discernible to the foot as Masters moved forward. The grass was still wet with dew and he parted it before him with his arms. There were saplings, too. Mostly horse-chestnuts with stems already over an inch in diameter and six feet high— the progeny of a great conker tree towering at the north-west corner.

Some yards in, Masters stopped and looked about him. Except over the top of the gate, he could no longer see the road. Another step to the right, and even this view was denied him.

"What are you looking for, Chief?" asked Reed, standing on what remained of the beaten track to the south door.

Masters replied slowly. "I find this place a bit sinister. Not enough to make me afraid, but enough to remove me from a neutral attitude towards it. Now that's probably me being fanciful after discovering a murdered man yesterday. But Tennyson was a Lincolnshire poet, wasn't he, Webb?"

"Yes, Chief," answered the DCI in amazement.

"And what do you know of his work?"

"*The Brook.* 'Men may come and men may go.' That one."

"Anything else?"

"The one we used to call the Lady of the onions when I was a kid at school. *The Lady of Shalott.*"

"Yes. Well we've lost two men who were such close mates they were like brothers. Now we've found one of them. And Tennyson wrote a piece called *In Memoriam,* in which one of the lines asks, 'Where wert thou, brother, those four days?'"

"And?"

"It was some days between Melada's disappearance and Belton's, wasn't it?"

"About ten?"

"So where was brother Melada during those ten days?"

Reed gasped. "You mean...you mean you think he's here, Chief?"

"Why not?"

Reed looked about him. "Where exactly?"

"That's for us to find out. He's obviously not down the well, otherwise Iliff would have discovered him yesterday. But this is a graveyard...."

Sergeant Iliff picked up Green and Berger at The Chestnut Tree a minute or two after Masters had left.

"Where to, Mr Green?"

"Nowhere, laddie, not for a moment." Green got into the car. "These fires you've been having. Tell me about them."

"Nothing to tell, sir."

"Come on, laddie. There's bags of it. In which order did they happen? How long between? What time of day? How far apart? What did the fire officers say?"

"Well, sir, the first one was reported by PC Bannerman. It was the second Thursday in June. I don't know if you remember, but it had been as hot and dry as anybody round here could remember and people were already talking about a coming water shortage—the one we've got now, in fact."

"If they were saying that," said Berger, "it would mean the fire-brigades couldn't cope, and that's almost a direct invitation to fire-raisers. That's probably why it started."

"As to that, I can't say. But I do know the public were asked to be careful and vigilant, and the force—particularly the country bobbies—were warned to be on the lookout for outbreaks."

Green—unusually for him—offered his cigarette pack

to both the two sergeants. "Right, lad. I've got the background picture. Now let's get down to details. And don't leave anything out."

"Wouldn't it be better to see Bannerman personally, Mr Green?"

"I will, laddie—if what you tell me warrants it."

Iliff accepted a light and then began. "Bannerman was cycling his beat. In the early evening, it was. He came on at six, and I suppose it would be maybe a quarter of an hour later when he rounded the spinney at Adthorpe's corner. You won't know where that is...."

"Never mind. Go on."

"It was then he saw the rick fire."

"No smoke before that? I'd have thought he'd have seen it miles away."

"No sir. Very little smoke. Too dry, you see. Just a great mass of flame two fields away from the road. Ricks are sometimes built out in the middle of nowhere, and this was several years old, so it was no great loss to the farmer, though I reckon he'll have got compensation."

"What happened?"

"Nothing much. Bannerman knew it was hopeless to try and save the rick. It had almost gone in any case. But there was danger to the nearby hedgerow and its trees and, of course, to the standing crops close by. So he needed beaters. He radioed in for help. And there was a car pulled up there—two young couples who had stopped on the road to gawp. He asked them to take a message to the farm, which was about half a mile down the road, in a dip. Farmer Clifford hadn't seen the blaze, but he rustled up a few chaps with shovels to stand by. They couldn't get close to put out the fire because of the heat, but they managed to stop it spreading."

"What about the brigade?"

"We told them, and they came. But there was no water handy and they reckoned it was safer to let it burn itself out rather than use what water they had on board."

"Funny attitude."

"Not really. Water was short. And they'd have had to run out hoses across two fields of young crops—or drive across them."

"I see. Then what?"

"Nothing. That's it. Bannerman saw nobody who could have started it, and the fire-officer couldn't say what caused it. There were no obvious signs of paraffin or petrol being used. It could have been a fag-end from a courting couple having a cuddle there, or spontaneous combustion even."

"Dead end, eh? Right, what next? A barn, wasn't it?"

"Two days later. On the Saturday. Early evening again and seven miles away from Farmer Clifford's rick, Farmer Cobb's barn was burned down. It was an old, ramshackle sort of building...."

"A bit like the rick?" asked Green. "Not worth much?"

"If you're thinking Cobb burned it down to get the insurance," said Iliff with some heat, "you've got another think coming, Mr Green. Cobb isn't like that."

"I didn't say he was, son," said Green soothingly. "Farmers don't have to get up to that sort of trick to earn a bob or two."

"Meaning?"

"Meaning there's as many fiddles as cows down on any farm and don't pretend there isn't. You never knew a farmer go without beef for Sunday dinner."

Iliff accepted this without comment. "Anyhow," he continued, "it was an old barn, plank-built and pitched on the outside, and that helped the fire to burn more fiercely than might otherwise have been the case."

"Did the brigade get to it?"

"Yes. They didn't save it, or course, because there was nothing much to save. But I got a report from the fire officer next morning. I went along there and he was doing his inspection after it had all cooled down. He said that in his opinion the fire had started, not inside the barn, but outside it, in the middle of the south-west side to be precise."

"Hottest point, was it?"

"That's right. And he said it had been started by a piece of glass."

"How did he know that?"

"He found it. It was a spectacle lens. He said it had been thrown on some inflammable rubbish piled against the wall and it had drawn the sun's rays."

"Concentrated them like a burning glass?" asked Berger.

"That's right."

"And what had the farmer to say about that?" asked Green.

"He said he'd have understood a bit of broken bottle being there, though he's pretty careful to see none's left lying around because of the animals. But he was flummoxed by a spectacle lens."

"So am I," said Green. "Who'd drop a spectacle lens without looking for it and picking it up? And in a place like that? If you've had to pay for a pair of glasses lately, like I had to for my missus a couple of months ago, you'd know they come too dear to be dropped on rubbish heaps."

"Did the fire-officer think it was arson?" asked Berger.

"Not really. He had nothing to go on. But I interviewed Cobb, his family and the farmhands. None of those who had glasses had lost a lens and Cobb was sure no stranger had been near the barn because it's pretty near the house, but it was Saturday and most of 'em had gone off after work. There was the old cowman left to do the evening milking, but he'd had to go out into the fields to get the animals, so there was plenty of opportunity for anybody to get to the farm unseen."

"Right," said Green. "There was a gap of another two days, was there, and then a vet's place went up?"

"Three days. The following Tuesday."

"Early evening?"

"Yes."

"Let's have it."

"It was a very strongly built wooden extension at the back of the vet's house. He used the bottom floor for waiting room, consulting room and office and he'd had this bit built on to house his full stock of drugs and to use as an operating surgery. The vet and his wife lived on the top floor."

"No kids?"

"Just the two of them."

"And where were they when the shop went on fire?"

Iliff grimaced. "The wife was out. She always was on Tuesdays. Went to see her mother or to play bridge or some such thing."

"And the vet himself?"

"He was called out. Over to Cratchett's farm, but...."

"But what?"

"Cratchett hadn't called him."

"You mean the call was bogus?"

"Apparently."

"How do you know there was a call?"

"We don't. That is, we can't prove it. But the vet's a well-thought-of man, and I reckon that if he really wanted to blow his place up to get the insurance he could have done it at a time when he was out on a real case and wouldn't have to rely on a bogus call for an alibi."

"Hold it, hold it!" growled Green. "Blow his place up? You mean explosives were used?"

"As good as. Next to his operating table he had two cylinders—one of oxygen and one of ether. Before the brigade could get the fire under control, those gas bottles exploded. Believe me there wasn't much left of that extension, and the back of the house was seriously damaged."

Green sucked at his partial denture for a moment before asking, "Could the fire officer say where the fire started and how?"

"He said it had been started internally. He couldn't be sure. Not after all the evidence had been showered for miles around. But he got the feeling that the heart of the fire had been just inside the door near to where the vet had his operating table."

29

"Close to his gas bottles, in fact?"

"I reckon."

"So whoever did it probably knew they'd explode."

"I didn't say that."

"No, but it's worth bearing in mind. Now how did our incendiarist get in?"

"He wouldn't have to. If he broke a pane of glass in the door he could toss some burning materials to the point where the fire officer reckoned the blaze started."

"Glass door?"

"There was a lot of glass in the extension. It was for operating in, remember. He needed the light."

Green exhaled noisily. "And I suppose there was a spring lock on the door."

"Yes. And a bolt, and a chain."

"All of which could be opened once a pane of glass was smashed, I suppose."

"Right."

"Won't they ever learn?" Green turned to Berger. "O.K. It's your turn to hand round the fags." After the sergeant had obliged, Green again addressed Iliff. "Right, lad. That's three fires. There's two more. Another rick and another barn."

"Spaced a couple of days apart."

"Serious, were they?"

"How do you mean?"

"Well, so far, we've only had one fire that did what you might call serious damage. What about the last two?"

"They were like the first two. Started in the early evening. An old rick and an old shed-like place near a crew yard."

"Near a what?"

"Crew yard. A crew is a herd round here. A yard where they herd cattle. Usually ankle-deep in muck."

"Don't go on. I can imagine it."

"Anything else you want to know, Mr Green?"

"Lots, laddie. Lots. Start her up. We'll go to the site of the first fire."

30

It was Reed who found it.

"Chief!"

His call from the south-east corner of the churchyard reached Masters clearly enough in the area near the south transept. It was even heard by Webb who was operating on the north side not too far from the well.

They both converged on Reed as fast as the terrain and undergrowth would allow them. They came up almost together.

"This looks to me as though it had been tampered with, Chief."

The long grass had dried off at that spot. It seemed that rough turves had been lifted and then replaced, but the disturbance in such dry weather had caused the roots to wither and the tops to die off. A weathered old tombstone had been tumbled slightly askew across the stricken area. Masters stared at it for a moment and then squatted to fumble among the stubble and the base of the surrounding stalks with his slim, brown fingers. He opened his hand to show his spoil. Crumbs of brownish clay.

"There's been digging here. Look in the hedge bottom, please, Reed."

The sergeant was barely a step away from the hedge. "There's quite a lot here, Chief. He must have thrown the spare he had left over into the dip, hoping it wouldn't be noticed before it was overgrown."

Webb said: "Lucky for us there's been no rain to green this lot up, otherwise we might not have found it so easily."

Reed said: "If you'd give me a hand to lift the slab clear, Mr Webb, I reckon we'd be able to lift those clods free by hand."

"Lift the stone," said Masters, "but leave the turves. We'll do it properly. Your constable, Mr Webb, can do the digging, if there is any to be done, and I want a photographer present. Dr Watling, too."

"It'll take time to get the pathologist here. And we don't know that there's anything in there for him to examine."

"I just squatted close to the ground. Get down there yourself and you'll get the stench of death in your nostrils."

As Webb bent to help lift the stone he exhaled through his mouth. "You're right, Chief."

Reed grunted as they threw the stone over: "He usually is."

It was over an hour before the turves had been lifted and the few inches of soil scraped away from the body. Photographs had been taken of the untouched grave. Now they were taken of the shirt-sleeved corpse before the doctor was allowed to examine.

"Fortyish," he muttered. "Male, of course, despite the hair. Buried—at a guess—about two weeks, probably longer. We'll be able to be more exact later on." He got to his feet. "No apparent cause of death from the front. Can I turn him over?"

Masters nodded. Watling gave Reed a pair of thin plastic gloves. "Here, put these on, Sergeant, and help me to roll him on to his right side. And take it easy. I don't want him coming to bits in our hands."

Watling himself manoeuvred the dead man's shoulders and head. When the body was half turned he instructed Reed to hold it as it was. A brief examination satisfied him. "Skull crushed in. See? I can palpate it." He demonstrated for Masters' benefit. "A heavy blow there, right on the occiput."

"Depression?"

"Maybe. But not just along one central line. I think there's an area of splintering, and it's my guess that it is roughly rectangular with the longer axis running across the rear of the obtrusive part of the skull, rather than vertically."

Masters nodded. "Confirm that for me, would you? It'll make a difference."

Watling nodded. "If I'm right, it could mean there was no weapon used." He straightened up. "He could have fallen—or been pushed—against one of these headstones."

"Very likely. Now, identity." Masters turned to Webb. "I'm pretty sure it must be Melada."

"It is. I've seen him often enough. His features and his style of dressing—those tall boots and flowered shirt."

"Right. Could you arrange for the body to be taken to whichever mortuary Dr Watling uses? And also arrange for him—as well as Belton—to be formally identified by their wives?"

"Before you see the women?"

"I think so. We're not out to hide anything from them."

"I'll get going," said Watling, picking up his case.

"Thank you, doctor. May I still ring you this evening?"

"At six. Not later. I'm going out tonight."

"Six."

"What are you going to do, Chief?" asked Webb, obviously anxious not to miss any of the action while dealing with the body.

Masters grinned. "Reed and I will have a look round here while you're away. There may still be something we've missed. Get back as quickly as you can. You needn't go to Lincoln with the ambulance, you know."

Webb grinned his thanks. "In that case, half an hour should see me here."

Masters and Reed waited until they were alone in the churchyard and the constable was back on duty at the gate.

"What now, Chief?"

"The church, Reed. The Church of St John the Divine in Oakby. It's like a magnet."

"You mean it's attracting dead bodies?"

"All churches have done that. God's acre: hallowed ground."

"Undesirable dead bodies, then."

"Nearer the mark. The violently dead."

"What are you getting at, Chief?"

"I want to know why."

"Because it's isolated and overgrown. You could kill and bury best part of an army in here without anybody

33

being any the wiser unless a police car happens to break down just outside and an inquisitive Detective Superintendent decides to pass the waiting time by peering down wells."

Masters shook his head. "Not so, Reed." They were walking slowly along the little path between the gate and the south door. "Remember the notice? The tombstone notice? It's been up there some little time. The paper is yellowed and the lettering faded, and the date on it is twenty-three days ago...."

Reed sounded excited. "And Watling said Melada had been buried a fortnight, give or take a day or two, and Belton had been put down the well much more recently than that, so whoever put them where we found them must have known the place would be visited and cleared pretty soon."

"Quite. Nobody could miss seeing the notice on the gate or—" Masters stopped at the heavy door of the little south porch—"or here," he concluded.

Another of the notices was attached to the old grey oak, with little rectangles of cardboard under the heads of the drawing pins. "They shouldn't have done that," said Masters inconsequently. "They would have to use a hammer of some sort to drive them into wood that hard, and when the notice is down, there'll be holes left. They should have used sticky tape."

Reed had no reply to this remark, so he waited for Masters to recollect his thoughts. He guessed that the Chief had simply made this observation to give himself time to marshal what he had to say next. He stood staring at the notice for a further few seconds before turning to the sergeant.

"There's got to be a reason why this churchyard has been used." He laid his hand on the stonework. "It knows the secret, Reed. We've got to prise the secret out of it."

Reed stepped back and looked at the building with renewed interest. He was insufficiently versed in architecture to know that the little church was basically perpendicular in style: Perpendicular with a certain amount of decoration due to some local or fashionable quirk at the time of building. But he'd seen enough of churches to sense there was something missing.

"There's no side bits, Chief. No side aisles."

"No clerestory," said Masters. Then seeing that Reed wasn't with him, he explained: "The little windows you see down the sides of the nave above the roofs of the aisles. They normally give light to the central part of a church, but this one hasn't got a clerestory because—I suppose—to put one in so small a church would have spoiled the aesthetic balance. As you said, there are no side aisles. The roof comes out to the side walls whereas, customarily, it would be supported on the pillars which separate the side aisles from the nave."

"There'll only be one row of pews each side of the centre aisle, then."

"I imagine so." Masters lifted the wrought iron ring on the door and turned it. But the door was securely locked. "I'd like to see inside."

"We'll have to, won't we, Chief?"

Masters nodded. "Sooner or later. We'll ask Mr Webb who holds the key."

"Why go to the site of the first fire?" asked Iliff.

"Begin at the beginning," replied Green solemnly, "and work your way through."

"Does that mean you've got some ideas about all of them?"

"I have," said Green decisively. "They were all started in the early evening."

"I told you that, Mr. Green. We hadn't overlooked it."

"Good. What conclusions did you draw from that?"

"That the fire-raiser was some nutter who was at work all day and only found time to have his fun and games after knocking-off time."

"Grand. And?"

"What d'you mean? And?"

"Was that all you deduced from it?"

"What else is there?"

"Well, now, where shall we begin? It's not for me to teach you locals your jobs, sergeant. But did you find out how the other fires—other than Cobb's barn, that is—were started?"

"The brigade said no paraffin or petrol had been used."

"That was all?"

"In this drought they've been too busy to make detailed investigations of minor fires."

"Understandable. But if you knew how Cobb's barn was ignited, why didn't you look for the same *m.o.* at the other places?"

"I told you, we did look at the vet's surgery."

"Leave that one out."

"Why?"

Green sighed. "Look, lad, you've had five fires. Four of them did no damage. You just described them as minor. Two ricks and two old barns, one of each on either side of a more serious incident. Doesn't that suggest something?"

Iliff looked perplexed. It was Berger who, from the driving seat, said: "Camouflage."

"Eh?" asked Iliff.

"Five fires. Two similar ones on each side of a different one. Your fire-raiser isn't a nutter. He doesn't like causing damage, so he sets fire to four old, useless ricks and barns to cover up his real target."

"You mean...all he wanted to do was get at the vet?"

"Seems like it."

Iliff turned in his seat to look at Green. "Do you go for this, sir?"

"Why not? It's logical. It's what I've been trying to get you to see for yourself. His real target."

"You think I should be looking for somebody who has a grudge against the vet? A farmer he's let down somehow?"

"That's a possibility."

36

"Meaning you don't think it's the answer."

"No, lad, I don't. If he wanted to have a go at the vet, he'd have to go at him, and that would be that. A state of anger serious enough to drive a man to blow up a house is a very direct sort of anger. It wouldn't consider disguising the blow with other fires. But somebody calm—without any anger towards the vet—who wanted to draw the wool over our eyes, he would light five fires to make us think we were dealing with a nutter."

"So why set fire to the vet's place?"

"Because the vet had something he wanted, laddie. Come on, sergeant. Think about it. He draws the vet away with a bogus call on the one night in the week his wife is out."

"I'm with you, sir. But why set fire to the place? Why not just break in and nick the loot?"

"Because, son, he didn't want anybody to know what he was after. He hoped—by raising five fires—that we would think he wasn't after anything except lighting bonfires."

Iliff said to Berger, "That's Adthorpe's corner and the copse just ahead. Turn left there. Bannerman was coming from the other direction, so you can see why the trees hid the view." The local sergeant turned back to Green. "Sorry, sir. You were saying?"

"Just this, lad. If we're right, it explains why all the fires were lit in the early evening. Chummy wanted to establish a pattern so you would link all five fires and go for the nutter theory. But it wasn't his work that imposed the time. It was the fact that it was only in the evening that he could be sure the vet's wife would be out."

"But why early evening? Anytime at night would do, up to ten o'clock or so."

"No, lad, it wouldn't. Not with his chosen method of starting the fires. If he was going to use a burning glass, it had to be while the sun was still strong enough to ackle and pollock. And don't ask why he used a burning glass, because the answer's obvious. Isn't it?"

37

"Nothing to carry around with him. No petrol or paraffin or candles."

"Not even matches," added Berger.

"Right."

"Pull in at the gate on the left," said Iliff.

"And," added Green, "there's one other thing. You can fix a glass, I reckon, so that it takes a bit of time to work. Just a few minutes, maybe, but long enough for you to get well away from the scene before there's any flame or smoke." He opened his door as the car came to a halt. "And, let's face it, son, if you saw a bloke near a hayrick and he didn't even have any matches on him you wouldn't nick him as a potential arsonist, would you?"

Iliff agreed and proceeded to lead the way across the fields to the blackened remains of the old strawstack.

Webb looked hot as he rejoined Masters. It was obvious he had been hurrying in order to miss nothing of what went on, and he had done what he had to do well within the half hour he had allowed himself.

"Who is the keyholder of the church?" asked Masters as the DCI came up.

"Ah! Now there you've got me. Normally, there'd be a verger, wouldn't there? But as this church is redundant there won't be verger or caretaker. So, I can only suppose the vicar will have a key."

"Vicar of a redundant church?" asked Reed. "That must be a soft number."

"The church may be redundant, but the parish isn't. This is Oakby church. The parish is Oakby-cum-Beckby. The vicar lives and operates from Beckby. Name of...let me see, now...Canning. That's it. The Reverend Walter Canning."

"I'd like to see him and his key. He should be present if we open up."

"Right, Chief. I'll ask the PC at the gate for his address, and, if I could have the car...?"

Masters nodded. "Reed will drive you. I'll have a little

think on Heberden's seat while you're gone."

Masters filled his pipe with Warlock Flake and sauntered round to the bench at the west door. As he sat in the warm, mid-morning sunshine, he tried to visualise what sort of drama could have resulted in the discovery of two dead bodies in a disused country churchyard—apart from the rude forefathers who had slept there for many years now.

Had the bodies been killed by the same agency? He thought not. In his experience, multiple killers were rare, but when they did go into action, their *modus operandi* was usually the same, or at least similar. Melada had died from a blow on the head. Probably an accidental blow caused by falling against a tombstone. Falling backwards. That argued a confrontation with somebody else. A savage somebody who had then buried the body. Belton had died from causes as yet unknown. But somebody had hidden his body, too. Would the same person bury one body and drop another down a well? Masters had a gut feeling—based on experience—that there must have been two people involved in the disposals. At different times! Two of everything...two bodies, two causes of death, two disposers, two times...he pulled himself together. Two times? Twice. No, not twice. Two different times. That sounded better. "For the sin ye do by two and two ye must pay for one by one." He shook his head. Not applicable to murder. But...what was that line? "Three may keep a secret, if two of them are dead." That was it. Three missing men, including Heberden. Two of them dead, here, in the churchyard. Heberden could be the third, the one keeping the secret. He would have to pay some attention to the missing landowner whose seat he now occupied. Strange to think that a man should provide a bench for rest in a churchyard and then people that same churchyard with dead bodies. Too strange for truth? Maybe. He shrugged mentally and made a note to keep it in mind. Meanwhile, as his pipe had gone out....

Webb and Reed found him still sitting in the sun: the

second bowlful of Warlock Flake dead, but the stem still between his teeth. He came to at their approach and got to his feet at the sight of their companion.

The Rev. Walter Canning was a man in his middle thirties. Though obviously one of the new brand of parsons, he was no trendy. He was dressed in slacks, brown shoes, and a faded blue shirt open at the neck. His hair was auburn and short enough to be unfashionable. He did not give the impression of having played rugger at college, but Masters could see him hiking the hills with a pack on his back, a pipe in his mouth and a small Bible in his pocket. Now he seemed very perturbed.

"Superintendent," he said in a worried voice, after he and Masters had been introduced, "Mr Webb has told me you have found two bodies—those of two murdered men— here, within the boundaries of the church."

Canning was so obviously distressed at what he had learned that Masters took him by the arm and urged him to sit on the bench. Masters then sat beside him.

"I'm sorry about this, vicar. But, upset though you must be, at least it must be some relief to you to know that what has taken place happened in the precincts of a church that is now no longer used."

"It is still hallowed ground, Mr Masters."

"True. And we shall bear that in mind during our investigations. That is why I asked Mr Webb to bring you here, as I understand this was a chapel-at-ease within your parish."

"Yes. Thank you. I am entirely at your disposal. Please tell me how I can help, though it would seem to me that there is little or nothing I can do—except possibly say a prayer over the remains."

"The bodies have gone to the mortuary."

"Of course. Do you know who they were?"

"Mr Webb didn't tell you?"

"No."

"Well, we haven't had them officially identified yet, so it would perhaps be wiser not to say who we think they are until we are sure. But I can say that to the best of our knowledge they are not from your parish."

"That is some comfort, though of course it shouldn't be, because they are still—or were—men."

"Just so, vicar. But now, you asked what you could do for us. I'm sorry to say we shall need to look inside the church."

"Of course."

"You have the key?"

"No. The keys are held by the publican in Oakby. As the church is for sale, it was felt that the keys should be available nearby. The pub seemed the place most prospective buyers would visit so we asked Tom Goodall, the licensee, if he would mind acting as custodian. Besides, Tom was once a churchwarden here."

Masters looked up at Webb. "Didn't you tell Mr Canning we wanted the key?"

"Yes, Chief. He called in at The Green Man to get them from Goodall. But they aren't there."

"Where are they?" asked Masters slowly.

Canning spoke. "Tom told me he had given them to Mr Alexander Heberden some days ago."

— 3 —

As Green, Iliff and Berger reached the hedge at the far side of the first field, it was easy to see the large, blackened area where the old rick had formerly stood. They passed through a second gate and made their way towards it. As they got closer, it was possible to make out the outline of the stack itself. The bottom two or three inches of charred straw were still in position, not wholly consumed. Iliff explained that the immense weight of straw above had, over the years, compressed this bottom layer into a harder, more compact and, therefore, less inflammable mass.

"I'll believe you," said Green. "But I reckon that if there was any moisture about—and there would be, even though there's been a drought—it would most likely be at the bottom. So it was probably the damp that stopped that last bit going up in smoke."

Iliff grunted, and they stood silent for a moment or two, looking at the irregular area blackened by the fire.

"Where's west?" asked Green.

"Yonder." Iliff was a countryman, and with the sun shining brightly he had no hesitation in pointing out what Green wanted to know.

"So the stack was lined up, roughly, north-west and south-east, would you say?"

Green took a moment or two to consider things. "A burning glass couldn't have been on the north-west end, because the direct rays of the sun never get north of west."

"This south-west side, then," suggested Iliff.

Green shook his head. "The sun would shine directly on it all right, but earlier in the afternoon. Our bloody fire didn't start till after tea, did it?"

Iliff said: "In that case, it must have been right on the corner."

Green grunted assent. "Unless our boyo tried to be clever and pulled a heap out of the stack and placed his eyeglass strategically on that."

Berger said: "I'll comb the corner."

"Right lad. Get down to it. I want every square inch for a yard every way of that corner sifted through with your hands. Take your jacket off and roll up your sleeves."

"I could do with something to kneel on."

"Hold hard," said Iliff. "There's a good thick stake in the hedge. It's leaning over, so it could be loose."

The baulk of timber was a split pole with the flat side wide enough to kneel on. Thus protected from the worst of the feathery ash, Berger, using a small stick as a probe, gently sifted the black and grey ash: inch by inch as though counting sand grains. It was a hot, dirty task and a slow one. Slow because Iliff had suggested that the beaters could have broken a lens to flinders and Green had retorted that in that case he wanted the bits, every one of them.

Iliff relieved Berger from time to time, and between them the sergeants had been searching for almost forty minutes when Berger looked up and asked: "How's this?"

He held the stick out towards Green. On it was dangling a piece of brass bent over at one end and flattened along half its length.

Iliff peered closely. "Earpiece," he grunted, standing up stiffly. "The brass that goes down the middle of the tortoiseshell—or plastic, I suppose. The covering must have melted away in the fire." He turned to Green. "So that's that. You've established a link between the incidents."

"You can't start fires with bits of brass wire," grunted Green. "I want the glass."

It was a further ten minutes before Berger unearthed

half a lens. He handed it up to Green without a word.

"That's it, lad. The proof we need. Get yourself up. You'll likely be able to get a wash at Cobb's farm."

"Cobb's?" asked Iliff in surprise. "We know we've got a firebug on the loose, and the way he operates."

"Aye, lad," said Green as they walked back to the car. "But haven't you wondered why that earpiece was there?"

"Not for any reason except that the fire-raiser was too idle to break the lens out of the frame."

"Idle? Hardly. Not a chap who was so methodical."

"Why then?"

"You can start a fire if you sling a bit of curved glass on to inflammable material and the sun happens to catch it. But to make sure—if you wanted to burn holes in paper like we did when we were kids, or to light the end of a fag—you'd have to hold the glass away."

"To focus the rays," agreed Berger.

"That's it. So I think our fire-raiser used that bit of brass as a distance piece for the lens, to hold it away from the straw so's the rays would be concentrated in one spot."

"I get it," said Berger. "You think the firebug just broke a pair of spectacles in half across the nosepiece. Then all he had to do was jam the hinge to make sure the earpiece would stick out. He pushed the other end into the straw so that the glass was a few inches away."

"Right, lad. And we'll try to prove it by taking a look round at Cobb's farm."

"But, Mr Green...." said Iliff.

"What?"

"If that lens was placed like you think, that rick would have started to smoulder within minutes."

"You don't say! Look, sergeant, I've been telling you for the past hour that the timing of these fires was important to whoever started them. He wanted them all to go off at roughly the same time of day—to mislead us. Whereas, I reckon the time of day was forced on him by the movements of the vet's wife. So it was no use to him if they didn't start to smoulder within minutes."

Iliff opened the field gate. "Then whoever did it wouldn't have a chance to get very far away before those fires were properly ablaze."

"Now you're beginning to think, son. So now you know what you've got to do, don't you?"

"Ask about at the site of every fire."

"That's right. Get your local bobbies asking questions."

"If he had a car, he could get a long way away in two or three minutes," said Berger. "In fact, he'd have longer than that. The straw might begin to smoulder in that time, but there wouldn't be a noticeable blaze for perhaps another two or three minutes. In quiet countryside like this it could mean he'd be a mile away before anybody noticed anything amiss—always supposing there was somebody close by to see it early on."

"There wasn't at this one," conceded Iliff, getting into the car. "It was blazing away before those four people in the car and the constable saw it."

The local man drove them to Cobb's farm where, knowing exactly what to look for and where—within a yard or so—to look for it, he and Berger again began to search. After raking and sifting for no more than five minutes, Berger found a twisted piece of brass wire, discoloured by the flames but, as far as they could tell, the twin of the piece unearthed at the rick fire.

"That's it, lads," said Green with satisfaction. "Go to the farmhouse and ask if you can wash up a bit."

"You're not going to the other sites?" asked Iliff.

"I'm not. Your lads can do that. Though you won't find anything at the vet's place."

"I told you that."

"So you did. Now, get cleaned up. I want to find His Nibs."

"Alexander Heberden had the key, had he?" asked Masters. "And Alexander Heberden is missing."

"What?" asked Canning. "Mr Heberden missing? Since when?"

"Do you mean to say the village grapevine hasn't been working, vicar?"

Canning shook his head. "I knew Mr Heberden was going away to judge at some agricultural show. I did hear, however, now I come to think of it, that he hadn't cancelled the milk, though that was unlike him, for he was a most thoughtful and considerate man."

"That would account for it," said Reed. "If everybody expected him to be away, nobody would remark on his absence."

"Missing?" asked Canning again. "Are you sure?"

"According to Mrs Heberden he is. She reported the fact to the police."

Canning stared at Masters with troubled eyes. "I am perturbed, Superintendent. Very perturbed. In view of the fact that you have found the bodies of two men violently done to death within the churchyard, and now Mr Heberden has gone missing while in possession of the church keys—a fact I am at a loss to understand—I fear the worst."

"The worst, vicar?"

"You have combed the churchyard for signs of a third body?"

Masters nodded. "Thoroughly. This morning. Not after finding the first body in the well, because we had no reason to suppose there would be a second corpse. But after finding the second man...."

"I see." Canning stared at Masters for a moment, as the idea came into his mind. "You sent for me...or the key, rather... because you feared there might be another body inside the church itself?"

"I had no reason to think so when I asked Mr Webb to bring you here. But now I know that Heberden was—or is—in possession of the church key, I think I have every reason to fear that he may be inside the church."

Canning glanced round at Webb and Reed in turn, as if seeking a rebuttal of Masters' words. All he got, in return, was the sight of two solemn faces. "This is too horrible to contemplate," he said at last. "Two dead strangers in the churchyard is enough, but one of one's friends dead in the church itself...."

"Cheer up, vicar," said Masters, in a kindly tone. "We may be mistaken."

"I hope so. Truly, I hope so. Heberden! A pillar of society, locally. And two others...nameless men, as yet...but still men." He dropped into silence. After a moment Masters got to his feet. "It's after eleven o'clock. The village pub should be open. I'd like a word with the landlord, and I think you, vicar, could do with a drink."

Canning looked up. "I really believe I could. But I'm not accustomed to resorting to alcohol for solace."

"You can't go into church to pray, vicar. The door's locked. So come along with us. A drink will do you good."

Canning needed no further urging, and a few minutes later he was introducing Tom Goodall to Masters.

Masters ordered drinks and while Goodall was serving them, asked how often Heberden had asked for the church key.

"Not often as far as I know. We've only let them out a few times in five years. More often in this last month than ever before." He passed over the vicar's whisky and pints of beer for the others. "A chap called...what was his name? A big chap with black hair and a foreign look about him. Foreign name, too, as I remember. Here, Mr Canning, you brought him here that first time."

"Who, Tom?"

"That foreign-looking chap. He wanted to see over the church. What was his name?"

"Ah, yes. I remember. His wife was called Happy. I'll always remember that."

"Aye, but what was his name? Mel something or other."

"Melada," said Canning. "John Melada. He seemed very keen on buying the church."

There was silence in the saloon bar for a few moments. They were the only four customers and there was nothing to say after this bit of news. The vicar was savouring his

47

whisky, unaware that the name he had mentioned had silenced his companions.

For an appreciable time it seemed as if they were all waiting for somebody else to speak. It was Masters who broke the spell.

"Thank you, landlord." He turned to Canning. "Shall we go on to the table in the window, vicar? We can talk more easily there."

The parson agreed, and the four of them sat in a circle. It was obvious that the whisky had helped to restore Canning's spirits, and he made no objection when Masters signalled to Goodall for another round to be brought before the purpose of the coming discussion was divulged.

They were alone again before Masters began.

"Tell me about Mr John Melada, vicar."

"I know very little about him. I only met him the once, and that by chance."

"Tell me about that one meeting, then."

"It was rather a prolonged encounter and, you might say, split into two parts."

"It sounds very interesting. Almost intriguing. So much so that I'd like to know every detail you can recall. In full. Leave nothing out."

"Treat us like a congregation. As though you were preaching an intricate sermon," suggested Reed.

The second double whisky had completed the job begun by the first. It had loosened Canning's tongue. Few men—always supposing they were not suspected of any crime—could help but be flattered by the close attention of the three policemen—one of them as eminent as Masters. When the tongue has been loosened by whisky and you are a parson who loves to preach to an appreciative congregation, and rightly recognising that you are not too bad an exponent of the art, then an invitation to give an address is as welcome as oasis water to a parched desert traveller. Canning went ahead without further urging. Extempore as it was, as he warmed to his subject, the vicar's cameo held his listeners unwavering attention. The man of the cloth turned thespian. He played all the parts. He closed his eyes for a moment, as if to recall every detail of some scene, and then started his story.

"It was a lovely afternoon in late spring. In late May, this year. I had gone to St John the Divine's..."

Webb leaned forward to interrupt, but Masters laid a hand on his arm to stop him. The questions could come later.

"...and had stayed there, half an hour or so, sitting in the sun on the seat we occupied today. I find the solitude there...not uplifting exactly...but to my liking. I suppose I had fooled myself into believing that I could compose a sermon there, but I confess my sojourn was more in the nature of an afternoon snooze than a creative period.

"I had an appointment in Oakby so, reluctantly, I left the seat. I had parked my car in the village, so I was to walk back. It was when I got to the churchyard gate—I was actually through it and was fastening it behind me— when the noise of hard-soled footwear on the road caused me to look up. An extraordinary sight met my eyes. Coming from the direction opposite to the one which leads to the village was a big, dark-haired man, carrying a young woman pick-a-back.

"Perhaps I should describe the couple to you, because apart from so unreal a mode of transport, they themselves were slightly odd. As I said, the man was big and dark-haired. All of six feet and broad-shouldered. A hooked nose—foreign-looking. His hair was unruly, and there was far too much of it for a man rising forty, as I judged him to be. I told you I'd heard hard-sounding footsteps. Small wonder. He had on a pair of tall modern boots in pale tan with thick, solid soles—the sort most men would have matured out of before reaching thirty. He also wore a sky-blue suit, the jacket of which had bellows pockets, epaulettes and a belt which he wore unfastened. And, or so it seemed to me, he laughed continuously—at virtually every word spoken, either by himself or others. But I only realised that after I'd been in his presence for a time. So I'd better move on to describe the lady he was carrying. He had his hands behind her knees, and her legs stuck out in front, so I was immediately aware of her shoes. Quite small and plain shoes. Almost like a school-shoe. Very scuffed. She had bare legs, a flowered summer frock, very faded and short, and what looked to me like a home-made blazer fashioned from the material of an army blanket dyed navy blue.

"She was a small person, though I didn't realise that until I saw her standing on the ground. But up on the man's shoulders her head was only on a level with his, and so I should have appreciated her smallness straight-away. But I was too taken by her appearance to notice her size. She was what my mother used to call mousey-fair, with hair as straight as a pound of candles. It was cut in a fringe in front and fell down on both sides as far as her chin: a little chin on an elfin face. It was as though a child was looking through a picture frame. And she wore spectacles. A great pair of dark-rimmed glasses the bridge of which had fallen down to the end of her little nose.

"When they saw me, she asked to be put down. I saw then that she was not a child but a young woman. I would have guessed, at first, that she was a young student existing on a minimum grant and determined to be defiant about her tatty appearance. But I learned different a little later on."

Canning paused and finished the last drop of his whisky. Masters gestured to Reed to have the glass refilled.

"You're doing very well, vicar. You certainly have an eye for detail. We meet very few people who would be able to give so comprehensive a description of somebody they had met only the once, and that some weeks ago."

"People are my business," said Canning simply, as though such an explanation were a good reason for acquiring an all-embracing knowledge of all whom he met. That he was not very far wrong in what was, after all, almost a claim to clairvoyance, was borne out by what followed. With his third drink in front of him, he continued his account.

"When I had recovered from my surprise at seeing the bizarre progress of the two who were approaching me and," Canning said somewhat shamefacedly, "being a parson and, therefore, being parsonical in my conversation, I greeted them with a reference that I hope will not escape you. A modern version of 'that's no burden, that's my brother,' was what sprang to my lips. In reply, the man laughed aloud and said: 'She's not my brother, she's my common-law wife.'"

Masters nodded to show he had understood. "Then what, vicar?"

"Another surprise for me. The man addressed the woman as Happy. 'Here, Happy, get down, girl.' And he bent to allow her down. I immediately said 'Happy? I don't believe I have encountered Happy as a Christian name before.' Then she started to pull my leg. She pushed the glasses back on her nose and asked: 'No, father? You've heard of Joy?'

"'I always took that to be a shortened form of Joyce.'

"'And Glad?'

"'Short for Gladys? Yes. You're joking with me.'

"'You think so, father?'

"'What is your real name? May I know it? Because you have given me an idea for a talk I am to give to the Young Wives' Guild in a few days' time.'

"'Ness,' she said very solemnly." As he said this, Canning gave what appeared to his listeners as a fair imitation of a solemn young woman.

"'Her mother was frightened by a monster.' The man found his own joke very funny and laughed aloud.

"'Ness? That's a diminutive of Vanessa?'

"'You're on the wrong track, father,' she corrected me. 'My daddy liked a poet called Lowell.'

"'I've heard of him. One of the quotations from his work is quite widely used in the church. Maybe you remember it? "Who gives himself with his alms feeds three, himself, his hungering neighbour and Me." The Me has a capital M and refers, of course, to our Lord.'

"'Yes, well! Our quotation went like this: "Cleverness

and contentedness and all the other good nesses."' She peered at me very shrewdly. 'When I was born my daddy thought I was clever and contented and had all the other good nesses, so he called me Ness—as there was only one of me.'

"'But surely you mean goodnesses, not good nesses.'

"'Read your Lowell,' she said.

"'I shall certainly try to obtain a copy of his works. But I am still unenlightened.'

"'Her mother, padre,' said the man, 'decided she couldn't call her baby Ness. So she chose just one of the nesses for her.'

"'Happiness? Of course. Happy! What a delightful little vignette! I shall be able to make good use of our little chat. This has been a really fortunate encounter for me. My name is Canning and I'm the vicar of this parish.'

"This information seemed to amuse the man greatly. He laughed immoderately and then said: 'You already know Happy. I am John Melada.' And that, gentlemen, is how I came to meet John Melada. The experience stands out very well in my mind, probably because of what followed."

Masters filled his pipe slowly. "You know, vicar, you have not only an eye for a scene, but an ear, too. Your reconstruction of your conversation with Happy and Melada was extremely vivid."

"I don't think I strayed very much from the actual dialogue," said Canning, slightly on the defensive, as though he imagined Masters might be accusing him of exaggeration. "Certainly I have conveyed to you the exact sense of the meeting."

"I'm sure you have, vicar. And I'm not only grateful for your information, but impressed by your performance. Do you think you can go on to tell us what happened after that? You have whetted our appetites by saying that what followed helped to write the details of the encounter indelibly in your mind, so we can't help but feel that what is yet to come will be the best—from our point of view."

Canning smiled. "You know your Browning, Mr Masters. One never thinks of policemen as larding their conversation with aptly turned quotations from the poets."

"We're a queer lot," said Reed, as though such a general remark explained all the various quirks and idiosyncrasies to be met with throughout the whole of the national police force.

Canning took a sip from the third whisky and continued his story.

"I asked the couple if they were visiting Oakby, but they didn't even know where they were. I explained that they were in the parish of Oakby-cum-Beckby and they told me that their motor car had broken down a few hundred yards away...."

"Ah!" said Masters. "Now there's a thing. We broke down near here yesterday. We visited the church to while away the time until help came, and that is when we found the first body."

"I see. I wondered how you had happened on St John the Divine's....But Melada explained they had decided to walk to the village for help. Unfortunately, he was a big man and Happy was a small woman, so she couldn't keep pace with him unless he dawdled. And that is why he picked her up and gave her a ride on his back. It seemed to be a nice gesture—a harmless bit of fun. However, I explained that there was no garage in Oakby, and scarcely a phone. That dismayed them momentarily, because Melada told me—and he was laughing as he said it—that he had hoped to ring a friend of his, somebody called Rex, to come and pick them up."

"Rex?" asked Masters quietly. "Rex who?"

"He didn't say, and naturally I didn't ask."

"Quite. Please go on, Mr. Canning."

"As they were in need, I naturally felt I should help and so I said that as I had my car in the village I would be pleased to give them a lift to the nearest garage— almost as some measure of return for our entertaining conversation. Melada laughed at my offer, and for a moment I thought he had turned it down, but such was not the case. He said, 'Let's go, padre.' He seemed always to call me padre, as though he might have been a former member of the armed forces."

"Or he'd perhaps been in jail," said Webb. "The chaplains—like army chaplains—are called padres."

"Surely not? However, I was not in a position to take them to a garage at that precise moment, so I said there was just one little difficulty and that was that I had a call to make in Oakby that would take me some time. I explained that this would mean they would be left hanging about in Oakby with very little of interest to entertain them. Melada immediately said that they would spend their time looking round my church. When I said that, strictly speaking, it was not my church, he asked if I meant I was a visitor.

"I spent a moment or two telling them that I am the incumbent of Oakby-cum-Beckby, but that the parish church is in Beckby, and so is the vicarage. You see, Mr Masters, St John's was a chapel-at-ease until five or six years ago. Services were held there regularly until that time. But the congregation had dwindled and there was no longer a curate in the parish, besides which, my predecessor was also given the neighbouring parish of Trackwell to look after. So St John's became a redundant church.

"Melada asked me if that meant—and I use his words—that the church had been put up for grabs. I replied that it was for sale as it stands. The Church Commissioners wish to dispose of it, as they do so many fine old churches. But, as I explained to Melada, few people would wish to take on a building such as St John's. Certainly it is of no use for commercial purposes in such an out of the way spot.

"Happy asked me why I was there if it was no longer my church and I told her I had walked up because I was a little early for my call. Melada broke in and asked me if I'd got there before time for tea and suggested I was hanging about because I did not want to miss my cup of tea and slice of fruit cake. He was so near the mark that I admitted the impeachment which amused him greatly. Happy, however, insisted on knowing why I had visited the church. I couldn't confess to nostalgia, because I never conducted a service there. It was closed just before my time in the parish, so when she suggested I had come to study what might have been I corrected her. What was, would be nearer the mark. You see, gentlemen, for me churches—especially old ones—are history books. Accurate ones, not text books fudged up by historians who, in trying to paint a broad picture, so often disregard the details to be had from such places as St John's.

"I told that young woman that I was making it my business to study, in depth, the history of my parish. By studying the records, tombstones, memorials, gifts and all the other relics of the parish, I am getting a picture of the forebears of my present flock. As I told Melada and Happy, it is inspiring to me to know that a male ancestor of the woman with whom I was to take tea that afternoon was a pillar of St John's over four hundred years ago. It is on record that he attended the Bishop of Lincoln of the day— who made a pilgrimage on foot round his see—as baggage man, supplying two cobs of his own for the purpose for a period which included three sabbaths. I told Happy that and she replied that she expected I was there, at the church, just to soak up atmosphere. Melada, who seemed to be either extremely perspicacious or a cynic, said he guessed I was there to snooze on a warm tombstone, soaking up the sun."

"Which is more or less what you confessed to us," said Reed.

Canning nodded. "I can't deny it. Nor did I deny it to them. But I was quite unprepared for Melada's next request. He asked if they couldn't see over the church, despite the fact that it was redundant. I replied that I hadn't got the key, but he said, quite logically, that if the property was for sale, the key had to be kept close by for the convenience of prospective buyers. To that I had no option but to reply that such was the case, and to say that to the best of my knowledge no prospective buyer had come forward.

"His reply took me aback. He said, quite simply:'Well, there has now.' I suppose I sounded a little stupid when I asked: 'You?' And then Melada said yes and Happy said no at the same time. At this direct divergence of views I turned from one to the other, seeking an explanation. Happy said Melada wanted to go inside the church, but not as a prospective buyer. She refused to say why she had said this, but Melada was quite adamant that he was serious in considering the purchase of the church and demanded to be told where the key was kept. When I told him that it was kept here, by Tom, he said he would walk down with me to collect it, and I could vouch for him. The girl said it was too hot to walk and decided she would wait in the churchyard until Melada returned with the key.

"And that was that, for the moment, Mr Masters."

"You mean you had no conversation with Melada on the way into the village?"

"We did not walk in silence, but all we discussed was the amount the Commissioners might accept for the property. I told him I had heard of one isolated church being sold for as little as two thousand pounds. I suggested he should visit the diocesan office in Lincoln and by that time we had arrived here. I got the key from Tom and handed it over to Melada."

"You were going to help them to get to a garage, remember."

"Oh yes, we made arrangements for that, too. Melada was to return on foot to the church and I would motor up there to collect them after my parish visit."

"Which you did?"

"Of course. I cut short my call in order not to keep them waiting."

"A short time ago you said your meeting with Melada

was in two parts. Was the second part when you went to pick them up?"

"Yes."

"They were in the church at the time?"

"Yes." Canning took another sip of his whisky. "At the altar. I went in by the south door, which they had left open. The inner door of the porch made no noise as I entered, and as you see, I wear rubber-soled shoes, so they did not notice my coming. But I was able to overhear something of what they said."

"Was their conversation interesting?"

"By that do you mean was it out of the ordinary?"

"Yes."

"No. But it gave me a chance—a lead rather—for airing my local knowledge, and as you have probably guessed, I like the sound of my own voice, particularly on my own subjects."

"Would you care to listen to your own voice telling us what you told Melada and Happy? It is quite important that you do so."

"I will take your word for it, Mr Masters, but please remember you have given me no reason for so prolonged a discussion, except that Melada was one of those who once borrowed the church key recently."

"Twice, at least."

"I don't follow."

"You borrowed it once and handed it to him. Tom Goodall said you brought him here the first time. Meaning there was a second time, at least."

"Are you sure?"

"Check with Goodall, would you, please, Reed."

Reed got up to call the landlord through from the public bar and ask his question, while Masters turned again to Canning. "Vicar, I said we would withhold the names of those bodies in the churchyard until we have positive identifications. But I will tell you now, in all secrecy, of course, that we believe one of them to be John Melada."

The vicar stared in horror.

Masters continued: "So you see now why I must know everything about your meeting with him."

"That poor girl!" murmured Canning. "Poor Happy! She will be so dreadfully unhappy now. I feel I should call on her, even though I imagine she is a Roman Catholic."

"She told you so?"

"No. But just as Melada called me padre, Happy called me father throughout our conversation. The usual mode of address in our persuasion is vicar or rector, whereas those of the Roman faith address their priests as father."

"You must wait until we are sure Melada is dead. We know he is missing from home. Perhaps you would be so kind as to offer to accompany Happy to the mortuary."

Canning inclined his head. "Anything I can do...."

"Thank you."

Reed returned. "Melada came again a second time to borrow the key. He had another man of his own age with him."

"Thank you, Reed. Mr Canning is just about to tell us of the second half of his meeting with Melada."

Canning looked up, his face showing the shock the news of Melada's death had caused him.

"The altar table in St John's is of stone," he said quietly. "It was built at a time when, I suppose, the altar frontals and cloths we know today were not in common use. And so the altar is, itself, intrinsically decorative. The top is a slab of stone supported by three pointed arches in the front and one at each end. No doubt you can imagine it?"

"I can," said Webb. "There's a deal of that greyish lime-stone round here in buildings."

Canning acknowledged the correctness of that observation with a lift of the hand that was toying with the whisky glass. "Melada and Happy were standing looking at the altar. The empty church was like a sounding board. I could hear their words distinctly as I came up the centre aisle. I think Happy was feeling less than pleased at Melada's interest in the church—or at least where it was leading. At any rate he had his arm round her. 'What's up,

Hap?' he asked. 'Look, I'll tell you what. You don't like this place, but I think it's got possibilities. Big possibilities. And I reckon I could make a packet out of it.' At that point I can remember her looking up at him and pushing her glasses back up her nose. They always seemed to be slipping down. Then she asked the one-word question: 'So?' His reply was: 'We'll do a deal. I want it, you don't. I'll let you fix the price I offer for it. Any reasonable figure you like. And that's the maximum I'll go to. If I get it for whatever amount you say, fair enough. If I don't get it, that's that.'"

"Did that mollify her?"

"I actually stopped to listen for her reply. It seemed important to do so. She asked: 'That's a promise, Johnny?' and he replied: 'It's a promise, Hap.' She seemed to accept that, and he bent down to examine the underneath of the altar table.

"Immediately he got down, he said, 'Here, Hap, there's a space under here.' She joined him, and he pointed out that one of the floor slabs had been moved. I think I should explain that below the table were four slabs, just like paving stones. Three were fitted perfectly, the fourth had been lifted and set slightly askew so that it rested on its neighbour, leaving a small triangular hole through which Melada was peering. They were too taken up with their discovery to notice me behind them."

"What happened next, vicar? Did you speak?"

"No. Melada grasped the slab and raised it. They're not too heavy, particularly as he pivoted it on its back ledge. What they saw was a regular hole, a couple of feet deep, stone-lined and the same size as the altar. I was quite amused by the conversation which followed. She asked what it was and he replied that it was what he'd always wanted—a sunken bath.

"But Happy demanded to know what it was for and Melada, of course, could not tell her. So then I had to make known to them the fact that I was present. I said: 'It was intended as a tomb.'

"Happy was startled, but Melada laughed and said there was no skeleton in it. So I had to explain that when I said intended I meant intended and not used. The first vicar of the parish had it prepared for his own. He wanted to be buried under his own altar."

"What stopped him?" asked Reed.

"He died of an epidemic in London."

"The plague?"

"I think not. But definitely something catching. It is referred to in the records very simply as the fever, but his family could not find anybody willing to carry his corpse from London to Oakby for burial, so I imagine there was fear of contagion. My research suggests that it was either typhoid or anthrax or at any rate one of the enteric diseases."

"Nasty."

"The clothes as well as the person would be infected, you see, so that anybody in close contact with either would have been in danger."

"So he never made it to his tomb?"

"Sadly, no. I explained all this to Melada and Happy. All Melada was concerned to establish was that nobody had ever used it as a tomb, so that he could persuade the girl that, being untainted by death, it would make an ideal sunken bath if tiled out in colours of her choice. Happy, however, wanted to know why it had never been used."

"You could tell her?" asked Masters.

"At length," replied Canning with a little, slightly tipsy laugh. "The Heberden family—"

"Hold it! Hold it!" said Webb excitedly. "You said Heberden."

Canning nodded. "Alexander Heberden, the man you tell me is missing, is of the same family as the old vicar. Not his direct descendant, of course, because he was a younger son and so went into the church. Alexander is the elder son's descendant. As you know, he lives in the old family house, or what remains of it, just on the far side of the village from the church."

"He owns the village?"

"Not nowadays. But he owns a lot of land between Oakby and Beckby. It is all good agricultural land of one sort or another and is well farmed."

"You told all this to the two in the church?"

"The bit about Heberden? Yes, sometime later. But when I was answering Happy's question about why the tomb had never been used, I told her that after the first vicar died, the Heberden family made a votive offering expressive of a desire to leave the tomb unused for ever. In return, the wardens of the parish hold certain properties in perpetuity, a fact for which I personally am thankful in that the income from the properties forms a not insubstantial part of my own stipend.

"Melada was on to that as quick as a flash. He wanted to know how, with the church for sale, the wardens could guarantee their half of the bargain. I explained that it was an easy matter because nowadays nobody is allowed to bury a body except in consecrated ground or other areas specifically set aside for the purpose. Now that St John's is no longer used as a church it would be impossible to get permission to inter a body in Heberden's tomb, unless the new owner of the property wished to store an urn of ashes there and that would not be quite the same thing as the burial of earthly remains. He heard me out and then asked how, if the church were to be sold, I could still claim the income. I pointed out that the offering was to the parish and so it remains, even though one church is closed. We are keeping within the spirit of the expressed desire and the letter of the law.

"Melada seemed satisfied and Happy told me what I already knew—that Melada wanted to turn the tomb into a sunken bath. She seemed so upset at the idea that I tried to reassure her by saying that he would have a difficult job on his hands as there was no water in the church. I told him there is a well just outside the vestry door, but explained one didn't need much water in a church except for the font and the flower vases.

"He laughed—as usual—and said 'I thought you watered the wine, padre.' I was a little surprised by his knowledge, but I explained that the small amount needed for wetting the two forefingers of the officiating clergyman's hands and for swirling in the chalice to make certain the last of the consecrated wine is drunk was very small indeed and would be brought to the church by whoever conducted the service.

"Happy, as I said, seemed pleased that there was no piped water, but Melada said all he would need was a pump. When I added that there was no electricity to drive a pump he said he would make his own with a second-hand compressor bought at an army surplus sale.

"At that point—because he seemed so very determined to buy the church, even against his wife's wishes—I said to him that I thought there was some inner compulsion driving him on. He'd brushed aside every objection. No water, no electricity and—as I pointed out—no lavatories either. His answer to that was that he would dig a septic tank in the churchyard.

"What could one do in the face of such determination? As I said to Happy, I didn't know whether to be pleased at his strength of purpose or—in view of her obvious unhappiness—to be sad at his wilful disregard of almost insurmountable difficulties and her feelings. But I did go so far as to say to him that I thought he should pay some heed to his wife's wishes.

"At that, Melada bent down and lowered the raised flag into its correct position. It was such a perfect fit that it fell home on its ledges with a faint plop as it compressed the air in the tomb. And as he did it, he told Happy that just to please her he would seal it with cement and move the altar so that he could put a sofa or sideboard over it.

"At that point I had to say that if they wanted me to take them to a garage they would have to cut short their viewing. And it was then that I told Happy about Heberden. She told me she'd seen the name on the seat outside while waiting for Melada to return with the key.

Melada locked the church, and catching the end of our conversation, asked if Alexander Heberden was a wealthy man. My reply was that I supposed he was comfortably off, but not nearly so rich as his forebears were, in comparison. I said a bit about taxation hitting men like Alexander Heberden even harder than it hit men like us. To my great surprise, Melada laughed and said he wouldn't know about that because he never paid any tax. I doubted that, but he said he didn't if he could possibly help it, and told me not to look so shocked. Christ, he said, wasn't very keen on tax-gatherers, was he? That bloke Matthew, who became one of His biggest buddies, had to jack in the tax gathering before he was allowed to become a disciple, hadn't he?

"I admitted that what he had said was substantially true, so he asked why he should aid and abet tax gatherers in their sinful ways by paying taxes. He reckoned he was doing them a favour by abstaining."

"Abstaining?"

"That was the word he used. He went on to ask me if that wasn't another thing we preached—abstinence. I could only reply that he was too good a theologian for me, and much as I would have liked to hear more of his thoughts about the church's teaching, I felt we must hurry away. And that, Mr Masters, is the end of the story. I drove them into Beckby and introduced them to our local repair man and left them to it. The conversation during the journey did not concern me. In fact, I was left out of it. The two of them carried on a conversation virtually as though I was not there."

Masters thanked Canning for his report and for his time. As the four left the table, Masters did, however, say that he may find it necessary to call on the vicar again. Canning assured him he would look forward to a future meeting and expressed himself as only too happy to help the police in every way, for, he explained, he did not want a ravening beast loose among his flock, killing and desecrating as it went.

— 4 —

It was after one o'clock when Masters and Reed reached The Chestnut Tree. They had dropped Webb who, declining their invitation to take a ploughman's lunch with them, had explained that he wanted to call in at his office to see what had dropped on his desk in his absence, but specifically to ask whether the bodies had been positively identified as Melada and Belton. Iliff, too, had driven home for lunch, leaving Green and Berger at the pub to await Masters.

"Beer and a salad sandwich," said Masters when Berger asked if he could order for him. "Half a French loaf split longwise and well filled with greenery and tomatoes. Get the same for Reed. We've had a session already this morning and we've both got a drop to soak up if we're not to sleep all afternoon."

"Boozing from eleven o'clock?" asked Green in amazement after being told what time the party had started. "What were you doing? Sitting on the doorstep waiting for them to open?"

"Entertaining a talkative parson."

"The joker from Oakby."

"The vicar of Oakby-cum-Beckby. The Reverend Walter Canning."

"He preached you a sermon?"

"For the price of three double whiskies."

Green looked at Masters. "For you to prime the pump that much, the sermon would have to be a bit different from most of those I've heard in church. Let's have a guess

64

at his text. How about: 'Ding dong bell, body's in a well.'"

"You're getting warm."

"So I should be, the number of fires I've raked out this morning."

"You sound as if you found more than ashes."

"And if the body in the well wasn't a big enough topic of conversation to occupy the mind of a sermonising parson, you, too, must have found a little something else to talk about."

"We found a second body. What did you find?"

"Two spectacle lenses and two half spectacle frames."

Reed and Berger came across to the table with four plates of food and then went back to the bar to collect the tankards.

"Our find was quite a spectacle too," murmured Masters.

"It would be. It would also be John Melada—at a guess."

Masters nodded. "He was under the sod. Literally. He had been buried just below the surface."

Green picked up his huge sandwich and said: "You know, when my mother saw us kids with a doorstep like this, she used to ask us if we'd got a sore hand. Only we always had mousetrap or a slice of boiled bacon in between. We lived well, you know." Having had his say, he took a huge bite at the bread. It took some getting through and took a moment or two to separate. As he pushed stray strands of cress into his already over-full mouth, he added: "Want to tell me what the parson had to say?"

"When we're all four settled."

Green chewed noisily and then gulped to clear his mouth. "I can't see what the parson would have to tell you that's so interesting, unless he knew Melada."

The beer arrived. Green took a pull. "Was he a pal of Melada's?"

"He met him once."

Green grunted and picked up his sandwich again.

Masters recounted the events of the morning and the interview with Canning. At the end, Green said: "He

65

mentioned Rex, did he? I'll bet you didn't tell Canning that the body in the well was Rex Belton."

"I didn't," confessed Masters. "I didn't want him too maudlin. I believe Melada's death was a real blow to him. A second one—in so far as he may well have claimed an affinity with Belton equal to that he claimed with Melada simply because Melada had mentioned Rex in his hearing—coupled with the three double whiskies, which I daresay is an unaccustomed amount for him, could have caused him to preach rather than instruct. And I didn't want that."

"You gave him the drink," accused Green.

"Admittedly. He didn't ask for it. I wanted to oil the cogs of memory, overcome any judicious reticence there may have been, and loosen the tongue. Though I needn't have worried about the last. He'd talk for free."

"To some purpose. If what he said about Melada wanting to buy that church was true there should be a good lead following up what happened."

"Agreed. Remember there were tombstone notices outside the church and as we've been told there hadn't been any other prospective buyer for years to have put them there, it could be that he actually went ahead with his idea despite his girl friend's objections."

"Could be. But I tell you what."

"Something I've missed?"

"What the two of them said in the car. The parson said they ignored him. I find that hard to swallow. When a chap's doing you a kindness, do you just leave him to chauffeur you about the countryside? I reckon you lean over backwards to include him and offer him sweets and fags. And, what's more, I don't believe that a chap who's as talkative as you've made Canning out to be would let himself be left out of any conversation like that."

"Go on."

"I'd want an explanation as to why he didn't pin your ears back with a full account of that journey."

"He said the conversation was unremarkable and that

Melada and Happy ignored him."

Green took a large swig of beer. "It's too easy."

"What is?"

"To say that and get away with it."

"A feeling. If a parson was party to a conversation he didn't think he should report to the police...."

"The secret of the confessional?"

"That sort of thing, yes. If he thought that, and could bull you along by giving you a full account of everything that went on earlier, then you'd think he was being entirely open with you and you'd accept it when he said the conversation in the car was unremarkable."

"Which I confess I did."

"Right. And so would I have done if he hadn't said those two had left him out of it. That last bit, as I've said, doesn't ring true to me. The parson's a talkative bloke, Melada's a jovial extrovert, and Happy is a little sweetie. That's the picture, isn't it? So how could Canning have been ignored?"

Masters looked thoughtful. Eventually, he said: "I'll buy that. It's a point that didn't occur to me. We'll call on Canning this afternoon. If he is keeping something to himself, we'll get it out of him. If not, we can just say we were passing and thought he'd like to know the identity of the man in the well."

"Devious bastard."

"You put me up to it."

"I know I did. Here, Berger, lad, more beer. On me." Green handed over a fiver and turned back to Masters who said: "You haven't told us about the fires yet."

Green sucked at his partial denture for a second or so before replying. Then he said: "I reckon we've uncovered a bit of well-laid-on hanky panky."

"To do with the murders?"

"No obvious link. But judge for yourself." He then ran through the events of the morning concerning the fires. When he came to the end, Masters said: "You've come to the conclusion that four of the fires were started to cover

67

the purpose of the middle one—the vet's surgery?"

Green nodded.

"I think you've read the situation correctly. It is right, isn't it, that the four cover-up fires caused minimum damage—financially, I mean?"

"No great loss at all. Two tumbledown sheds and two old haystacks."

"So the target was the vet?"

"Don't you think so?"

"Not necessarily."

Green said: "You've got a better idea?"

"How about what the vet had in his surgery? Could it be something from there rather than an effort to embarrass the vet himself?"

Green digested this for a moment. "Maybe," he conceded. "But how will we ever know that?"

"By questioning the vet himself. About any enemies he may have and about what he kept in his surgery."

"You want me to do that?"

"Only if you want to. We've got a lot of interviews ahead of us. I want to see Canning and the wives of the two dead men. Then there's the diocesan office and Mrs Heberden. I'd prefer you with me."

"Fair enough. How about Reed, Berger and Iliff sorting out the vet while we get on with the interviews?"

"Webb will be with us."

Green shrugged. "We'll need somebody to show us the way."

The vicarage at Beckby was an old house standing in a lot of ground. Webb, who was driving, pulled up at the double gates and the three of them got down to walk up the drive to the house. They were approaching from the side, level with the front building line of the house. To their right were trees, some of them very old, which gave way to the front lawn of the house. To the left of the path was the kitchen garden. This area, at least, appeared in good shape, and neat rows of onions, lettuce, leeks and all the other customary vegetables were showing well.

"The parson's been digging for victory," said Green. "It looks to me as if he won't do too badly in the grub stakes if he gets through that lot."

"I'd say he sells some," said Webb. "The clergy aren't well paid, and if you've got the land and can make a bit on the side...."

"On the principle that God helps them who help themselves?"

"It would be practical Christianity, wouldn't it?"

"If he declares his earnings it would."

Masters said. "There's a woman coming through the gate from the back of the house."

The backyard, with outhouses, was walled off from the kitchen garden. The woman who came through the gate—a sad, once green affair needing a coat of paint—appeared to be in her early thirties, wore slacks and a sweater covered by a plastic bib apron and carried a trug full of garden implements and gloves in one hand and a kneeling mat in the other.

"Mrs Vicar?" murmured Green.

"I imagine so. Hang on." Masters went towards her and selected one of the tracks of beaten earth between the vegetable rows to get where she was. She had seen them and stood waiting.

As Masters approached, she said: "If it's the vicar you want to see, I'm afraid he's not available."

"Mrs Canning?"

"Yes."

"My name is Masters. I'm a policeman."

"Oh! You're the one investigating the bodies in St John's?"

"Yes. I spent some time with your husband this morning. Could my colleagues and I have another word with him now, please?"

"Well...."

"He's not busy writing a sermon, is he?"

"Not exactly."

Masters had a hunch. "An afternoon nap, perhaps?"

She smiled. "How did you guess?"

"Two clues. First, if he was on deck he'd be out here helping you and, second, as I was guilty of tempting him to have a drink before lunch, I suspect he would be feeling a little sleepy on an afternoon like this."

"So you're the one who did it. It certainly isn't like Walter to drink much at any time, but before lunch...you'd better come in. Do you mind the back way?" She went to the gate through which she had entered the garden, pausing to wait for Green and Webb to join them before passing through. The yard was of red brick, old and worn where feet went between the doors of the outhouses and the back door of the house, but covered in a faint green moss in corners and off the beaten tracks, as though nobody had taken a bass broom and given it a good brush-up for years.

The back needed paint. The narrow hallway inside needed paint, paper and carpet. Where this passage broadened out, past the stairs, into the main hall, there was a large square of coir on the floor, two bentwood chairs and a bamboo hall-stand that looked as if it had been left over—if not from a church jumble sale, at least from the white elephant stall of some function connected with the parish.

Mrs Canning led the way into what she designated the vicar's study. It *was* his study, but it was also—patently—the family living room. Masters had visions of young Mrs Canning being forced to beat a retreat to the kitchen whenever her husband received callers on private business. He was there now. The chair he occupied was high-backed and winged and covered in faded and much patched chintz. But it was old and comfortable. It was obvious from the way he occupied it that it had been tried over long years as a nest of rest and had never been found wanting. The vicar was sunk into it, with his legs straight out in front of him, ankles crossed, shoes kicked off. He was blissfully asleep. He had a peaceful air about him as though his whole being knew that, being a good man, he could enjoy the sleep of the just.

"It's a pity to wake him," said Green, his sarcasm heavy enough to drive piles through granite. "Let's go away and leave him to sleep it off."

Masters shot him a glance of exasperation and hoped Mrs Canning would pay no attention to his colleague's words. He need have had no worry. Mrs Canning woke him with a kiss. "Come along, old sleepy," she said, planting the kiss on his forehead. "You've got visitors."

Canning woke with difficulty, as if drugged. When he recognised Masters and Webb, he struggled to sit up straight and to put his feet into his shoes at the same time.

"I wasn't expecting to see you again quite so soon, Superintendent. Please forgive...."

"Nothing to forgive," said Green. "If I'd had the chance I'd have had a zizz myself after lunch on a hot day like this."

"Detective Chief Inspector Green, vicar," said Masters.

"Oh, hello. Please sit down."

There were plenty of places to sit—of one sort or another. Mrs Canning chose a pouffe, although she referred to it as a humpty, which Masters privately thought to be a far more attractive name for it. "May I stay?" She asked nobody in particular, but in a voice which intimated that she proposed to do so, come what may.

Green said: "We're not going to eat him, you know."

She gave him a look which suggested that she didn't really know whether she could trust Green not to go that far. But it was clear she was there to protect her mate from men who had already proved—by giving him too much whisky—that they didn't have his best interests at heart.

"Please stay, ma'am," said Masters. He turned to face Canning. "Vicar, this morning you told us that during his conversation with you on the afternoon you met him, Melada mentioned another man."

"Did I?"

"The friend whom he wished to phone to come and pick him up."

"Oh yes, I remember. Rex somebody or other."

"Rex Belton."

"I didn't hear the surname."

"The name of the man whose body was recovered from the well is Rex Belton."

The vicar's face showed his sorrow at the news. "His friend, too? I take it you are saying it is the same Rex?"

"Rex Belton and John Melada were close friends."

"This is dreadful. He was...murdered, too?"

"He was dead before he went into the water, and dead men don't throw themselves down wells."

"Couldn't he have...died near the well and when he...collapsed...have somehow fallen down the shaft?"

"Chance in a million," grunted Green. "In ten million, in fact."

"I see."

"Vicar," said Masters after a pause, "I know you regard these two deaths as a great tragedy but we, as policemen, regard whoever caused them as a menace who may not yet have finished his grisly work."

Canning nodded miserably. "Fiend," said his wife. "Whoever has done it is a sacrilegious fiend."

"You must of course take that view," began Masters.

"No," said Canning. "Whatever he has done, whoever he may be, he is one of God's children. Not a fiend, my dear. Fallen, but not a fiend."

Masters again seized his chance. "My concern, vicar, irrespective of your view of the killer, is to protect the living. To this end, I want you to tell me, in the greatest detail, what transpired during the conversation which took place in your car whilst you were driving Melada and Happy to the garage here in Beckby."

Canning shook his head doggedly. "I told you I was not involved in the conversation. Nothing of note was mentioned that I can tell you about."

"Ah!" said Green. "I don't believe you, vicar."

Mrs Canning, scandalised, turned on Green. "How dare you?"

Green was not abashed. "You heard, Mrs C. I don't

believe your old man. Look at the facts for yourself, love. Your old man is a great talker. He loves the sound of his own voice. Do you really believe he could keep quiet for yoinks while his two new friends chatted away?"

"He said he was left out of it by them."

"Think again, missus. Your hubby is doing a kindness to two extrovert people with whom he's just been gabbing twenty to the dozen in the church, and they ignore him in the car?" He switched to the vicar. "Which of them was sitting next to you?"

"He was."

"Laughing, smoking, chatting?"

"Yes."

Green turned back to Mrs Canning. "Your old man is a good parson. He doesn't like telling lies. He tried to qualify one just now. He said: 'Nothing of note was mentioned,' but then he added, 'that I can tell you about.' Well, it's not because his memory's bad. He's proved that. So it must be that he thinks what he heard was privileged information."

"My husband is a minister of the church. Like lawyers, much of what they hear is...."

"Don't stop," said Green. "You were going to say sacrosanct. Or something like that. Like in a confessional."

"Yes."

"So you do think your husband heard something that day. Something detrimental to Melada. Something that he can't tell us about. Well, I'll tell you something. I agree with you, love. But his attitude is a load of bunkum. Melada is dead. So is Belton. They can't be hurt by anything that's said now. But probably somebody else can be saved. That's what it's all about, isn't it? Parsons save their souls? Policemen save their lives? Come on, tell him to open up."

"Why should I?"

"For the best of reasons, love."

"What's that?"

"Because we don't know and you don't know if he isn't

73

to be the next victim. Let's face it, the murderer has certainly got some sort of fixation about that church, and nobody's closer connected to it than your old man."

Green had frightened her.

"Do you really think my husband is in danger?"

"I've just said we don't know. If we did, we wouldn't be here asking questions. We'd be out there putting the joker in question behind bars."

"If my husband answered your questions, how would it help?"

"He may give us some fact to help us identify the murderer. Some bit of knowledge he doesn't know he has. But any information about the victim could help us find the killer. That's all we want."

"No," said Canning decisively. "Not a word."

"Excellent, vicar, thank you," said Masters, getting to his feet. "So definite a refusal to speak can only mean that you did learn something that day and you think that whatever it was was of so serious a nature as to be equivalent to a confession. And I can't help but remember that confessions are usually admissions of sin or guilt."

"You twist words," accused Canning.

"It's better than twisting necks," said Green brutally. Then he changed his tone. "What are you holding back? The fact that Melada incriminated himself in some way? To say so wouldn't harm him now. In fact he could purge himself of his guilt—if that's the right phrase—through you, if you were to act as his mouthpiece now and so help to prevent further crime."

The vicar shook his head, not firmly, but indecisively. "I don't know. I just don't know."

"Try a bit of muscular Christianity," suggested Masters. "Don't be indecisive. Be active in doing good."

He seemed to have struck the right note with Canning, who asked: "If what I have to say is not... not relevant to your case, will you assure me that it will be kept secret?"

"As quiet as the grave," said Green.

"But some graves don't remain silent, as we know," Canning reminded him.

"I promise you absolute discretion, vicar," said Masters. "Absolute. We shall take no notes nor will we make any subsequently. And if we have to use your information, overtly that is, I shall consult you before doing so."

"In that case, I'll take your word."

"Thank you. Now is there a lot to tell us? If so, I suggest you emulate your excellent performance of this morning so that Mr Green can judge what a reliable raconteur you are. I sang your praises over lunch, and I believe he thought I was exaggerating your powers."

Canning brightened considerably at this verbal applause. "There is quite a lot to recount. I'd better do my best to recall everything so that any elusive fact which may be lurking there will come out, even if it should not be immediately recognised."

"Good," said Green. "Do you mind if I smoke? No objections? Have a fag, Mrs C." Green held out the crumpled packet.

"No thank you. But there is an ashtray on the mantel."

When they were finally settled, Canning began.

"Melada sat in front with me. Happy was at the back, leaning forward with her arms resting on the backs of our seats for the most part. Melada smoked. He rolled his own in dark brown papers, which were unfamiliar to me but which he said were liquorice flavoured.

"As we started up, I asked Happy how old she was and she told me she was twenty-eight. I expressed my surprise—I thought she was little more than twenty—but Melada laughed when I said so and then he declared she had been his mistress for more than four years."

"Did she deny it?" asked his wife.

"No. But this increased my surprise because I would have said she far out-ranked him in intelligence, so I asked what she had done before meeting Melada and she replied she had been too busy taking a first class degree in zoology and wild-life conservancy to worry too much about the mating habits of men. Her words, not mine. But it began to dawn on me that they were totally companionable. They totally accepted one another. And this, too, surprised me, because I judged Melada to be a womaniser. I hinted as much to him. It was Happy who replied.

"She said—in so many words—that he was a great womaniser: an accomplishment not entirely due to his own volition." Canning looked across at Masters. "And it was at that point that I virtually dropped out of the conversation. All the verbal exchanges thereafter were between the two of them, although much of what was said was addressed to me."

"I understand, Mr Canning. Please go on."

"Happy said that women just went for Melada in a big way—personable and physically attractive women. So most of his friends were surprised that he lived with her, Happy, who was—she said it self-deprecatingly, you'll understand—far from being a woman of striking beauty. His friends were not surprised that Happy had consented to team up with him, in view of his magnetic attraction for women, but they were surprised that she had stayed with him for so long because he had, while making no effort to conceal the fact, conducted affairs with at least half a dozen other women during the period of his relationship with Happy.

"I was really too dismayed to ask questions. Country folk are probably as promiscuous as people like the two I was with, but they don't parade it—flaunt it, almost. Melada however joined in and gave me an unasked for explanation. The essence of what he had to say—with much laughter—was that their friends didn't fully realise that in Happy he had found what so few men are lucky enough to find: a girl from the exact mould to suit him mentally, physically and sexually. That is why he had stayed with her and she with him even though he constantly fell from grace due to the blatant opportunities offered to him by other women. And I certainly got the impression, Mr Masters, that because of her suitability for him, Happy could manage Melada—something I imagine no other woman had ever been able to do."

"Would you say, vicar, that one of Happy's qualifications for the job of Melada's mistress was that she was as sexually voracious as he appears to have been?"

"If I had to guess, I would have said undoubtedly. Not that she said anything salacious in my hearing, but she had what I can best describe as almost a possessive air, full of sexual promise. I don't know whether that will convey anything to you?"

"Most graphic, thank you, vicar."

"She told me that Melada did everything with a laugh. She had noticed that I glanced at him from time to time during his outbursts. She said it was both his saving grace and his downfall. People liked him because he never appeared to take himself seriously, but had he been more temperate he could have been considered an able man. He never, apparently, stuck at anything for long, so that—as he put it—his list of jobs and enterprises was almost as long as the catalogue of women he had seduced.

"She confessed that in many ways he was lucky. Happily extrovert, he interviewed well. He had always managed to get himself a job when he tried—even, apparently, jobs for which he was totally unqualified. But he never kept one. It seems that employers found him out quite quickly and then, apparently, it was a toss-up as to whether they grew disenchanted with him before he grew disenchanted with them. Whichever happened—according to Happy—they always parted company on the best of terms and, as a consequence, Melada had a host of acquaintances, all of whom regarded him as a likeable rascal. And that, she said, suited him admirably because whenever the need arose—as it often did in his life—he always knew somebody who might help with information he wanted or—and here I'm guessing—who could suggest some course of action which might be profitable to someone like himself not possessed of too many scruples."

"You got the impression he was unscrupulous?"

"In business? Yes. As you will hear later, I think I have reason for my view. I think Melada would have made use of his best friend for profit—and then laugh it off."

"Did he say what work he was doing at the time?"

"I got the impression he was resting between ventures. And that is why St John's attracted him so greatly. Also, he said to Happy that he would like to get a mature student grant to read law."

"He what?" grunted Green.

"It surprised Happy, too. She asked what he thought they would live on while he was studying and he replied: 'Whatever you can make, love—plus the eighteen hundred I'd get.'"

"May I break in?" asked Masters. "Did Happy say what her job was, if any?"

"There was no mention of it. Not even a hint."

"Thank you."

Canning continued.

"She accused Melada of having looked into the business of mature student grants without telling her. He laughed it off, but then said he'd met a snag, and that was that even if he got the grant and a place at university the legal professions would never admit him."

Masters said: "Stop there, vicar, if you'd like to. If it is easier for you, you needn't tell us the reason. We can guess. The reason why a man would be debarred from a career in law is because he has been convicted of some crime. I suspect that is what you were uneasy about telling us."

"One of the things," admitted Canning.

"I'll get on to records," said Webb.

"Apparently it was for fraud. He did time. Happy told him she always knew his past would catch up with him and then said—and again I quote—'You only got off the last time because the fuzz hadn't quite enough evidence.' To which he replied quite blithely: 'True. Enough to put me in court, but not enough to put me inside.' Then he went on to say that we have a good legal system here. He admired it and that's why he would like to join in. He said that when he thought how much he'd paid his lawyer, he reckoned he personally could make a fortune at it.

"She said that if the principle of setting a thief to catch a thief held good he'd make a sensation as a criminal lawyer because he could certainly do the necessary talking to be a real mouthpiece. And that was the end of that particular bit of chat. The subject changed. He said it was because he couldn't read law that he proposed to buy St John's."

"What on earth for?" asked Green.

Canning's face clouded. "I must be honest with you and confess that I can't decide whether what followed was a hoax—an attempt to pull my leg—or whether they were serious. It was so difficult to decide with Melada laughing aloud at everything, whether humorous or not."

"We can appreciate the difficulty," said Masters, "and we will bear it in mind as we listen."

"I sensed—and I believed my feelings to be true at the time, and I still do, with the proviso I have just made— that when they got on to the subject of buying the church, Happy was . . . well, unhappy. I think she thought her man was obsessionally bent on buying St John's."

"He'd told her she could fix the price," Masters reminded him.

"Even so, I think that she herself had experienced a love-hate relationship for the old church and she was filled with foreboding. That may sound as though I was exaggerating in the light of what has since happened, but she stated in that rather serious little drawl of hers, that never before had one of his proposed ventures caused her concern, and they both knew that some of those had been hairy enough at times." Canning looked across at his wife. "Please forgive some of my language, my dear, but whenever possible I am using their words."

She smiled at him. "You're doing very well, Walter. Isn't he, Mr Masters?"

"Very well indeed. I'm sure Mr Green will bear me out and he is famous for his memory. Almost total recall."

"True," said Green, with no false modesty.

Canning continued.

79

"Being an intelligent woman, I believe she sought a reason for her disquiet and failed to do so. I also believe she recognised that the weapon of fixing the price he should bid that he had offered her, with such apparent magnanimity, was a dangerous one. Fix the bid too high and she would beggar them; fix it too low and she would lose the man because, despite his laughter, even I could see that Melada was so desirous of owning the church that he would regard with distaste anybody who prevented his acquiring it were this to happen."

"You think that was the root cause of her unease?"

"Not the root cause." He paused. "Mr Masters, you must understand that I am interpreting what I heard. Interpolating my own thoughts, if you like. I could be entirely wrong."

"We shall, of course, bear that in mind, Mr Canning. But we feel we ought to hear everything you have to say. When a case is thrust upon us, literally out of the blue, we have to probe and listen and then, finally, sift what we have learned. With too little to work on, we get stuck. At least, if there is too much, we are never short of lines along which to enquire."

Green grunted his agreement and lit another cigarette. Canning glanced across at his wife for her approval before continuing.

"I would have said that well-read and intelligent though she obviously was, Happy was not extremely imaginative. I put her down as a level-headed type, rather placid in thought, who would take very few, if any, mental leaps in the dark. What I mean is that I believe she could write a first-class factual essay in her subject, but she could never have fathomed the reasons for actions and then propounded them as a tenable theory. I think flights of fancy were beyond her. She was not whimsical. I would say she had never been susceptible to any psychic or spiritual influence and yet my impression at the time was that she could foresee that for Melada to attempt to buy the church would be a disaster. She certainly tried to tell

80

him so, but he laughed and told her she had the last word in that she could tell him what to bid next day."

"Next day?"

Canning nodded. "Happy was surprised, but he said he intended to go into Lincoln first thing because there was no point in waiting. Then she asked—finally—what he intended to use it for as they certainly couldn't live in it. His answer was that he proposed to turn it into a studio to hire out by the week or month for people who wanted to get away from it all for a bit, to paint or write or just for a holiday.

"She said he'd get no takers for a church with a grave-yard round it, but he laughingly told her he wouldn't leave it like it was. He said there were thousands of things to do. Rooms to be made, graves to be moved...."

"At that point she said, 'Don't, Johnny. Please don't.' But he simply asked her if she were scared. She replied that yes, she was scared, and when he asked her what of, she said she didn't know and that was what scared her. She again demanded to know why he was so dead-set on acquiring an empty old church in the middle of nowhere and he replied by asking why she was so keen to stop him.

"Her reply was that the answer to his question was easy. She literally just didn't want to buy trouble. But he hadn't answered her question and she continued to insist on knowing why he wanted the church."

"Did she ever get a reply?" asked Masters.

"He laughed and said: 'Don't ask me. I just want it.' She asked: 'Like a child wants a toy?' and he replied: 'If you like.' At that, she said he would tire of it in no time at all and they would be left with an unwanted church on their hands, but he still persisted in saying he wanted it. She again asked him for what purpose he wanted it, but he still didn't reply. At length she asked if he had some reason for wanting the church that he wasn't revealing to her. A dishonest one, perhaps. He denied this, but I think she got near the mark when she asked: 'Kinky, then?' It seemed to me that his mood altered for the worse at that point, and he gestured to her to keep quiet. She took the hint, but she had the final word."

"Which was?"

"'If you buy that church for the purpose I think you want it for, Johnny Melada, I'll kill you.'"

There was a short silence after Canning had finished. Then Masters said: "I see now why you were reticent, vicar. You thought that by telling us this, you would be pointing an accusing finger at the young woman, Happy."

"Yes," said Canning miserably. "Isn't that just what I've done?"

"I can't give you an answer. Maybe yes, maybe no. Ask yourself whether a slightly built young woman could somehow murder two fully grown men and then dispose of their bodies. If you think it is possible for her physically to do this, then you may feel that you have pointed a finger at her. If not, then you haven't. We have been more than interested in your account, and I have no doubt your impressions will be extremely useful, but in the end, we shall deal with only proveable facts."

Canning sighed with relief. He had given no proveable facts. As they left the vicarage, Green said to Webb, "Didn't you check to see if either of those two jokers had a record?"

"No, I didn't," said Webb. "I suppose I should have done, but I haven't got round to it. Not that I've had much time since yesterday afternoon. That's not my excuse, though."

"No? What is?"

"First, because I suppose I'd always look to see if somebody I thought was a criminal had a record, but it wouldn't usually occur to me to check on a victim."

"I see what you mean. But it doesn't always work that way, laddie. Villains get chopped as often as honest people."

"Not in the sticks. Not usually, at any rate."

"I'll take your word for it. And if that's the first reason, I suppose there's a second?"

"The obvious one. If Melada has a record, I'm surprised I haven't heard about it."

"Nuts," said Green, getting into the car. "We're always having to get on to CRO to check on villains in the Smoke. We can't remember everybody's petty details."

"This is a sparsely populated area, and fraud doesn't sound petty to me." Webb started the car and had moved off before remembering to ask Masters where he'd like to go.

"To the diocesan office in Lincoln, please," said Masters. "I'd like to check up on Melada's transactions and to collect the spare keys of the church which are held there, according to Canning. Whilst we're there, Mr Webb, check with the Lincoln people about Melada's record. See if they know anything about him or Belton which we ought to know."

"Right, Chief."

Green was never sufficiently at ease in a car to snooze, though Masters would have loved to doze in the heat of the mid-afternoon even though he had comparatively little to drink, and for so big a man, a relatively light lunch. He supposed that listening closely to two lengthy sermons from Canning in one day might be cause for slumber. But Green was not prepared to let him rest.

"Wonder how those sergeants are getting on?" he asked as the car went down a leafy lane which, though wide enough for two vehicles, still seemed too narrow for comfort.

"I imagine it will depend on how busy the vet is. If he's operating out of makeshift premises and every dog owner for miles around is calling in because little Bonzo has got sun stroke...."

"He does a lot more large animal work than pets," said Webb.

"Horse doctor, is he?" asked Green.

"Horses, cattle, pigs. 'Course he does run surgeries for pets. That's what puts the jam on the bread and butter."

"What's his name?" asked Masters.

"Marchant," replied Webb.

"Any other vets in the area?"

"A fair sprinkling. There has to be in rural areas like this. Animals can't wait for attention if they're sick any more than humans can. Losses come expensive to farmers."

"Does it matter how many there are about?" asked Green grumpily.

"Perhaps not. But if Marchant finds any difficulty in telling Reed and Berger exactly what he had in his surgery cum dispensary, perhaps they could get some idea by calling on a neighbouring vet and looking at his stocks and equipment."

Green grunted his agreement, and the car started to run into the outskirts of Lincoln. Now that the hedgerows were not as high they could see the huge square towers of the cathedral rising impressively from its hill. "The Raf bomber squadrons used to use that as a collecting mark during the last struggle," said Green. "When there was a thousand bomber raid on, the first of them had to get up into the air quite a while before the last ones in the wave. They circled Lincoln cathedral while they waited to form up. It showed up, even at night, you see. And I bet they were damned glad to see it when they were coming back, too."

Webb added: "These parts were one big airfield," and then fell silent as he negotiated the city traffic. A few minutes later he dropped them at the diocesan office and went off to the local police station.

The secretary of the Diocesan Redundant Churches Committee was a retired Brigadier called Alton who, to supplement his pension, had taken a job on the accounting side of the see's secretariat. His office was small and smelt of dust, though it appeared clean enough, as though the Brigadier had it ready for inspection at any time. Masters guessed that the smell came from dust that was ingrained, having lain undisturbed for decades on papers and shelves before Alton had moved in and given the place a spring clean.

"Melada?" said the Brigadier. "Remember him well. Jovial type. Always laughing. Felt myself that it wasn't good nature as much as something he couldn't help. Like a nervous tic. But he seemed decent enough and pretty clever, I thought."

"We found his body—dead—buried in the churchyard of St John the Divine in Oakby."

"You did what?" The Brigadier stared up at Masters. "Here, sit down, Superintendent. And you, Mr Green. Smoke if you want to. Found his body there, did you?"

"You knew he was dead?" asked Masters.

"Missing. His little missus came in here asking if I'd seen him or had any dealings with him in the few days before she came."

"And had you?"

"Not in that period. Before then I had."

"What about telling us all about it?"

"Nothing to tell."

"Come on, Brigadier," said Green. "Report in full. From the moment you first saw him to the last bit of business you did with him. Particularly as the business was to do with St John's, wasn't it?"

"Entirely."

"And that's where he's been found, dead and buried. And as dead men don't bury themselves, we've got to have information so's we can discover who did him the courtesy of putting him underground."

"In that case, I'll give you the facts."

"We wouldn't mind a few impressions, too," observed Green. "When relevant. How did he strike you—that sort of thing."

"Understood. When he came in here, that first morning, I'd have said he was a bit shamefaced—though you might not have believed it by his laughing demeanour—at arriving to offer only two thousand pounds for the church. He obviously half expected me to send him packing with a flea in his ear."

"Which you didn't?"

"Of course not. When you've got umpteen purpose-built

buildings on your hands, all in out of the way places and no longer being used for the purpose for which they were built, what do you do? I'll tell you. You sit and wait for somebody to come and buy them. But the years pass, and nobody does come. So you don't turn your nose up if a chap bowls in and offers a ludicrously low sum. You can sell some of the urban churches, of course, for warehouses and the like. In fact one has been turned into an electrical power sub-station and several into theatres and concert halls. But that's by the way. Nobody wants a warehouse or a theatre in the back of beyond, without water, light and heat. So, I say, when somebody like Melada comes along and offers—well, not exactly peanuts, but certainly a sum less than munificent by today's standards—we grab at it."

"You mean you accepted his bid on the spot?"

"I accepted his bid, but I couldn't sell him the church on the spot. The bid had to be sent to the Church Commissioners in Millbank."

"What would they do?"

"Jib at it. When you're sitting in the middle of London where prices are astronomical, it takes a great deal of mind adjustment to accept that anybody who offers two thousand pounds for a church and two acres of ground is serious."

"So Melada was unlikely to get his church?"

"That's what he thought when I told him much the same as I've told you. But I told him not to be too despondent. I explained I wanted to clear my books so I undertook to write 'em a letter which—after they'd come up for air—would paint the real picture."

"Did Melada offer cash?"

"Oh, yes. Mortgages aren't easily come by for dilapidated churches."

"Did he tell you what use he intended to put it to?"

"I insisted on knowing that, because we sometimes get a bit sniffy about handing over former consecrated premises for what we think to be unsuitable purposes. We tend to favour museums, libraries, theatres and the like. The arts, as it were."

"What were his plans?"

The Brigadier leaned forward and took a large envelope from one of the drawers in his desk. "The fellow was something of a draughtsman. He had come prepared with a couple of pen and wash sketches of his proposals. He said he proposed to convert it to a studio for artists, writers or pop-group rehearsals. I was a bit shattered by that last, but as he explained the church is totally isolated and so he would be doing the community a service. Mind you, I don't think community service was uppermost in his mind. Some of these leading groups will pay the earth for the hire of a retreat for a week or two while they work on perfecting their horrors. But what he said was more or less in line with what the committee consider suitable uses."

"Are those his sketches?"

"Yes. He left them with me to support his case." The Brigadier took two pieces of drawing paper from the envelope, and laid them on the desk for Masters and Green to see. "They impressed me, and I told him so."

"Very good," agreed Masters, "especially as he had only seen the church for the first time the afternoon before."

"Have you been inside St John's?" asked the Brigadier.

"Not yet. The key in the village is missing. As I understand you have a spare here, I'd like to borrow it."

"That's easy. But why is the one from the village pub missing?"

"Because the man who last borrowed it is away from home and presumably has it with him. At any rate he hasn't returned it."

"I see. I'll look into it. Now these sketches. Would you like me to describe them, seeing you're unfamiliar with the terrain?"

"Please do."

"This one is a view from the south-west corner, from just to the left of the south door. You see Melada sketched in a balcony running the whole length of the opposite wall. There are no pillars in the church, so he has placed upright wooden beams to support it. Notice how it cuts across the windows at the point where they start to arch. By doing that he gets natural light on both ground floor and balcony. Of course the balcony is railed, but you see between the windows he has put bookcases and sofas. Below the balcony is the proposed dining area: see, he has a refectory table end-on to the wall and two halves of a pew—sawn ends hard up against the wall, as dining seats."

Masters picked up the sketch for a closer view. The Brigadier said: "There was to be another balcony above the head of the viewer. To take two bedrooms. Access was to be from the balcony above the chancel."

It was all there. A flight of stairs leading up from the chancel steps to the chancel balcony. The front three or four of this were curtained off to provide a landing running both ways to side balconies. Behind the partially opened curtain was the deep recess room which ran back to the east window.

"Bathroom?" asked Masters.

"In the chancel behind the stairs."

"Kitchen?"

"You're looking straight at it. In the robing vestry straight opposite you. Next to the dining-room area and next to the bathroom to save on plumbing and drains."

"And very close to the well in the churchyard."

"Quite. Close to the water supply."

The rest of the ground floor was given over to the living area. Melada had sketched in sofas, rugs, large pottery vases and a coffee table.

"Impressive," murmured Masters. He took up the second sketch. "This one, I take it, is looking west from the chancel steps."

"Roughly. From the south end of the steps, just under the pulpit."

Melada had made it look attractive. Green, looking over Masters' shoulder, said: "I can see now why he wanted to have it. For quick sketches these have been done with as much loving care as if...."

"As if what?" asked the Brigadier.

"I was going to say as if he'd intended staying there for life," replied Green. "I should have said for ever."

Nobody commented. Masters returned to his inspection of the second sketch. The chief interest was centred on the ringing chamber which was simply the rectangular space below the tower. There was a step up to it—a platform which protruded like a tongue into the centre aisle, on the end of which stood the font. Melada had proposed a balcony here, too, of exactly the same shape as the tongue. To reach it, he had proposed an upright ladder with tubular handgrips. The flight was anchored to the tongue at the bottom and the balcony at the top. Up above there was a child's bedroom. Down below, he had sketched in a seat which ran round the three walls of the ringing chamber and placed a small rug to occupy what remained of the floor.

"He'd decided to keep the west door closed?"

"I asked that question. He said there was the south door with its porch for the main part of the house and the vestry door for the kitchen. He proposed to seal the west door to keep out draughts." The Brigadier returned the sketches to their envelope. "I told him I would keep these well-hidden because they showed the possibilities too vividly. Anybody, on seeing these, would realise that refurbished in the way he suggested, that property would become valuable. Desirable, as the agents say. And then what would happen to the price? It would shoot up astronomically." The Brigadier put the envelope back in its drawer.

"Then what?"

"We discussed the outside. He'd got plans to turn the churchyard into a garden—lawn, flowers, fruit and vegetables. I told him, of course, that before he could clear the graves he would have to display a tombstone notice."

"We saw two copies at the church. Did he do it?"

"Oh, yes. It is a legal requirement, where former grave-yards are to be put to other uses, that the notice must be displayed for twenty-eight days warning of any intention to clear the land of tombstones. The notice gives interested parties a chance to know what you are about and to object if they wish."

"What happens if somebody does object?"

"If the objectors are close relatives of somebody buried recently, then the body must be disinterred and reburied in consecrated ground elsewhere."

"Exhumation!" exclaimed Green. "That would cost a bob or two."

"No coffins are opened. Just dug up and transported."

"At whose expense?"

The Brigadier grimaced. "Legally, at the expense of the church."

"So Melada was all right on that score."

The Brigadier shook his head. "I said legally. But with Melada offering as little as two thousand for St John's, I knew the Commissioners would make it a condition of sale that he should foot the bill should there be one. Either that, or they would insist on the tombstone notice being displayed for its full time before completion of the contract, just to be sure there was no expense to the church itself. I told Melada this."

"If there were no objectors the sale would go through. If there were objectors the price would go up?"

"The church has always had its cake and eaten it."

"What was Melada's reaction when you told him this?"

"Philosophical. He asked me to try, in my letter, to persuade the Commissioners to let him display the notice straight away so that he could see how he stood. I agreed and suggested that his best plan was to let our diocesan lawyers draw up and post the note for him so that there should be no slip-ups. As it is more or less a standard document I told him it would cost him no more than a few guineas."

"He agreed?"

"Yes. It was all done from here."

"And that was that?"

"He wanted to know how soon the deal would be fixed. He seemed impatient when I asked him to give me at least a fortnight before he next got in touch with me, by phone. We move with measured tread, Superintendent, and I was not at all sanguine about having news for him in a fortnight. That is why I told him to ring rather than call in."

Iliff had returned after lunch expecting to pick up Green and Berger. Instead he found Reed waiting for him in Green's place.

"That's better," said Iliff. "Your DCI gave me the run around! We've learned that the fires were started with spectacle lenses. But we're no nearer knowing who did it."

"No?" asked Reed, who had heard Green's report at lunchtime.

"No. Not a hope."

"It all depends how you look at it. My chief thinks there's something interesting about your fires, and he's asked me to follow it up. So I'd like to go and see this vet whose place exploded."

Iliff stared at Reed. "He's not suggesting Mr Marchant blew up his own surgery? Because if he is, I think he'll find he's mistaken."

"I don't know what he thinks, but he's not often mistaken. Not for long at any rate."

"OK. Get aboard. We'll go find Marchant, if he's available. He could be out at a farm."

"Where's he working from?" asked Berger.

"The front of his house. It was only the extension at the back that got the chop. The full brunt that is. The fabric of the house is still safe enough to live in."

It took just over twenty minutes to reach the vet's house in the little village of Wrigby. Iliff drew up outside the gate with its professional brass plate. "This is the front

91

way in—the private way. The normal entrance to the surgery is down that eight-foot at the side. There's a side door in the house."

"People didn't go into the extension?"

"No. Into the waiting room by the side door. Waiting room, consulting room and office are all in the house. He operated in the extension and kept his drugs there, too."

"We'll try the front," decided Reed. "It's not as if we were attending surgery."

Marchant was a tall, rangy man in his early forties. His girl assistant who answered the door to the three sergeants called him from the office to meet them. He wore heavy brown shoes, dog-toothed check slacks and a white, short-sleeved nylon jacket. He had a great deal of wavy brown hair, decently cut, but distinctly unruly. His face was lean and weather-beaten and he had blue eyes that carried a twinkle that matched the humorous quirk of the lips.

"Scotland Yard? For a country fire-bug? You're slipping, Sergeant Iliff. I'd have thought you'd have caught the nut without calling in the Yard."

Iliff reddened under this mild ribbing. "As to that, sir, we'll have to see. But the Yard team is here to deal with the business in Oakby you've no doubt heard about."

"They're surely not connecting me with it?"

"No, sir," replied Reed. "We're not. But this is a particularly peaceful part of the country. You get very little except petty crime and I've no doubt you're pleased about that."

"We are. Gives Sergeant Iliff an easy life, doesn't it, Sergeant? An outbreak of foot-and-mouth causes about our biggest scare."

"And that is a rare event, sir?"

"Thank heaven!"

"Then you won't be surprised to learn that if, simultaneously, you have an outbreak of fire-raising and an outbreak of murder all on the same little peaceful patch, we should want to make sure whether or not it is just a coincidence or whether there is a connection between the two."

"I see what you mean. But...outbreak of murder?"

"We've found two bodies so far, sir."

"Two? I heard of one. Here, I say, you're not expecting more, are you?"

"We hope not. But where there are two—" Reed shrugged his shoulders—"there may be more already, or there may be more to follow."

"You mean five fires, five deaths?"

"Hardly that, sir. But we have to be prepared for anything, so would you mind, first off, telling me if you have any enemies that you know of?"

"Who would set fire to my surgery, you mean? No. Not one. I've had a few disgruntled clients in my time, if they think I've let an animal that could be saved die on them. But that has always worn off after the insurance has been paid, and certainly none of those people would go to the length of burning me out."

"Well now, sir," said Reed, "that is just what Sergeant Iliff said of you. But if you have no enemies, what did you have in your surgery that somebody might want to get hold of?"

"Nothing of any value to a layman. There were a few fairly valuable instruments, I suppose. Even an X-ray machine. But nobody would want to pinch them. What gives you the idea that theft was the motive?"

"Revenge or theft, sir. Look at it this way. There have been five fires of which yours was the middle one. All the others have concerned old hay stacks and old barns— property of no value. But yours—well that's different. A house. And not just any house. A vet's house. And not just any part of that vet's house. His surgery, no less. Am I making myself clear, sir?"

"Yes, but even so it could be coincidence."

"Not a chance, sir. Whoever set fire to your surgery had to choose his time. The only time when he could be sure your premises would be empty. That meant after the working day—after your assistant had left the premises; and at the one time in the week when your wife is certain to be out. You, yourself, could be got out of the way at any time by means of a bogus call. But all this means that it was the attempt on your premises which decided at what time of day all five fires should start. With the others, timing was unimportant. So, sir, you'll see that if the incident here was the one by which the others were timed, and it was the only one where valuable property was attacked, it seems reasonable for us to suppose that either you were the target, or you had something the fire-raiser wanted."

Marchant raised his eyebrows. "Whoever it was didn't come here to pinch anything. He came to set fire to it and blew it up in the process."

Berger came in at that point. "That may be true, sir, but there is a different interpretation."

"What's that?"

"That the fire was started with the intention of causing the bottles of gas to explode in order to cover a theft."

"To make us believe nothing was taken, you mean?"

"It's feasible, sir. To disguise the fact that there was a break-in and a theft."

"I suppose that could be true."

"It is almost certainly what happened. The fire was started close to the gas. How else could that have happened unless somebody had broken in?"

"They could have smashed the glass in the door and thrown a lighted bundle to where the bottles were."

"Possibly. But would you like to put your arm through a broken window to throw a flaming bundle of rags accurately at a target, or would you even trust yourself to get near that target?"

"Frankly, no."

"And tell me, what sort of a flaming bundle could you trust to keep alight and burn long enough to achieve your object? In the short time, that is, before the vet you had sent off on a fool's errand discovered he'd been hoaxed and returned to put the fire out?"

Marchant looked impressed by Berger's reasoning. But he shook his head and said: "I still don't know why they picked on me."

Reed said: "It's my guess that you're the only vet within fifty miles that has a glass-panelled door to his operating room."

"Oh, lord!"

"You see, sir, they might not even have found it necessary to unlock it. Break a glass panel out of a door and you leave a hole big enough for a man to squeeze through normally. As long as he removed the splinters of glass, that is." Reed looked closely at Marchant. "Can you remember how the glass was fastened into the frame, sir?"

The vet nodded. "Putty outside and battens inside."

Iliff snorted. "Nothing easier to clear," he said. "Bust the glass close enough to the edge to prise a batten out, and the rest is easy. You clear as you go. No more than a two-minute job."

"So, sir," said Reed, "we'd like a comprehensive list of everything inside your surgery."

"You must be joking," said Marchant. "There were hundreds of items in there."

"Nevertheless, sir, we want to know. The big items should be easy."

"I've already listed those for the insurance people. I can give you a copy."

"Good. Now how do you propose to claim for your drug stock?"

"A blanket estimate. It's not itemised down to the last horse pill."

"Probably not, sir, but I'm sure you can remember most of what you had. You have an office?"

"In here." He pointed to a door on the right.

"Invoices?"

"Mostly at my accountant's."

Reed was not to be beaten. "Drug lists from suppliers, sir. And whatever you call your equivalent of that monthly index of specialities that doctors have. We'll go through them all, and we'll take down what you can remember having. You'll not find it too hard if you visualise your surgery shelf by shelf, and your poisons' cupboard, sir?"

"Of course. It was a locked, wall cupboard...."

"Metal?"

"Wood."

"I see."

"You sound disapproving. I was within the law, you know. A locked receptacle within a locked room. Just the same as when we have to leave a bag in a car. The bag has to be locked and the car has to be locked. But I needn't tell you how easy it is to break into a car—or a locked bag."

"No, sir, you needn't. Shall we go into the office and start the job?"

— 5 —

Masters filled his pipe slowly as the Brigadier brewed a pot of tea himself. He brought the pot and cups out of a cupboard and a saucer with half a lemon on it from inside an old box file that was lying flat on a shelf. "No milk, I'm afraid. I've taken to lemon because milk always goes sour and I was faced with getting rid of what remained and then washing the bottle because I don't like disposing of useful items. Don't like throwing tonic bottles away." He cut off three thin slices of the lemon with a little saw-edged kitchen knife. "Can you take it with lemon, gentlemen?"

"Suits me," said Green to Masters' surprise. "Used to drink it iced in Cairo."

"Ah," said the Brigadier, pouring the tea. "I take it you became partial to it stewed over a petrol fire with a matchstick in it to draw the smoke?"

"That's right! We used to tap the sides of the old brew can to make the tea leaves sink. There was an art in it. But then there always is in producing the earthly equivalent of nectar."

"May I butt in?" asked Masters, accepting a cup. "We've got a bit of sergeant major's brew to deal with in the case of Melada."

"Sorry," said Alton. "The old and bold tend to run on. Back to Melada. As I told you, we undertook to post the notices and we did so inside a couple of days. Melada had been back to the church and had seen them before he rang me at the end of the fortnight I had stipulated."

"Were you able to tell him he had got the church?"

97

"No."

"Why not? Some objection after the notice was displayed?"

The Brigadier squeezed his slice of lemon against the side of the cup with his teaspoon. "No. I told him that I thought his insistence on posting the notice before the sale was completed had turned out to be bad tactics. I hadn't realised it would be, and so to some extent I was responsible for his disappointment."

"What disappointment?" asked Green. "Don't tell me somebody gazumped him?"

"Not quite, because his bid had not been accepted. But displaying the notice gave other people ideas. And, as I knew they would, the Commissioners jumped at a higher bid."

"How much higher?"

"Five thousand. Two and a half times as much."

"Who by?"

"I am not sure I need to tell you that, as the negotiations have so far been cloaked in some secrecy. What I mean is, that the purchaser has been working through a third party."

"An agent, you mean?"

"Agent, yes. But if you mean house agent, no. I said third party. It was done to preserve anonymity and I can see no reason not to respect that."

Green, who had been sitting quiet, chipped in: "Some property tycoon getting his claws in, I suppose?"

"A man of property, certainly. But not a tycoon."

Masters said slowly: "A man of property? Now, let me see. Who is the person of whom we've heard mention— in connection with this case—as a man of property?"

Green gulped. "Alexander Heberden!" He turned to the Brigadier. "The local squire. Don't tell me he came in to buy the church?"

Alton nodded. "How you managed to guess is not my affair, but his family has been connected with St. John's for several hundred years and he disliked the idea of it passing into hands other than his own if the Commissioners were intent on selling it."

"Sentimental reasons only?"

"Purely. Or so I was informed. He proposed to turn the churchyard into a garden of rest and retreat."

"No plans for the church?"

"Vague ones only. I believe he was toying with the idea of recreating festivals—rural ones mostly—which now have been virtually forgotten."

"How d'you mean?" asked Green. "Maypole dancing and all that lark?"

"I imagine so. Going up the church tower on Ascension Day, which was an old custom. All Hallows Eve junketings, Shrove Tuesday pie suppers, egg rolling at Easter—that sort of thing. Some of them pagan in origin, no doubt. Others probably druidical."

"Sunrise at the solstice?" asked Masters.

"Could be. But I understand he was going to go for even bigger events. He aimed at giving Beckby a Passion Play. Like Oberammergau. To take place at Easter. Nativity play at Christmas, too, for local consumption, and in the summer a festival of church music. His idea was to centre the thing on the Cathedral choir and to augment it every day for a fortnight with different choirs from the diocese, ending up with some massive choral work."

"In a church that size?"

"I've told you as much as I heard, but I gathered St John's was definitely to be the hub of the affair. He probably envisaged using huge marquees in the churchyard, as I believe they sometimes do at Eisteddfods."

Masters pursed his lips.

"You've got to know quite a lot."

"I'm a nosey old man and I stick to the soldier's creed. Time spent in reconnaissance is seldom wasted."

"But you didn't see Heberden himself?"

"I insisted—as I did with Melada—on knowing to what purpose the church would be put. It had obviously been discussed, even if only in general terms, between Heberden and his agent, and that agent did a good selling job with their proposals. Certainly it provided me with good material for the Commissioners and, since they agreed to the sale, they must have approved."

"This agent," said Green. "Or third party. Who was he? Solicitor?"

"No."

"Just a moment, please," said Masters. "Brigadier, when we came and told you we'd found Melada dead in the churchyard, you were surprised."

"Of course I was."

"But this morning's paper carried news of a body found there yesterday afternoon."

"Did they? I read my leader page this morning and did the crossword at lunchtime, but I didn't see mention of a body being found."

"I suppose not," said Green. "The sort of paper you read wouldn't splash it across the front page. A discreet little paragraph somewhere would mention a body down a well...."

"Well? St John's well? Melada was found in a well? What had he done? Fallen down the shaft?"

"Not Melada," answered Masters.

"But you just said...."

"That Melada was found dead in the churchyard."

The Brigadier looked bewildered. "Forgive me, but I'm not sure I understand what you're saying. When you say in the churchyard, do you mean down the well?" He answered his own question. "Obviously not because you just said Melada did not fall down the shaft." He paused a moment and then looked across at Masters, startled. "Good God, you don't mean to say there were two bodies?"

"One down the well, a second in a shallow grave."

"Was one of them Heberden? You said you'd heard his name mentioned in connection...."

"Not Heberden."

"That's a relief at any rate."

"Why?"

"Why what? Oh, I see. You think I said that because Heberden is buying the church. No! Not that. It's just that one doesn't like to hear of any person one's heard about or done business with coming to a sticky end."

"I see. Just a general remark. Now, about the agent."

"What about him?"

"He was not out to preserve his anonymity. There can be no reason why you should attempt to withhold his name."

"None whatever. I had no intention of doing so. He was a man called Rex Belton."

The silence which followed seemed to cause Alton some unease. He looked from Masters to Green and back again. "Is something wrong? Have I said something that I ought not to have done?"

"No," grunted Green. "You've only confirmed what me and my Chief have been suspecting for about twenty minutes now."

"Oh? What's that? Rex Belton?"

"Little Tommy Thin," muttered Green.

"Little.... Who pushed him in? You mean...the nursery rhyme. Ding dong bell! Belton? Belton was the one down the well?"

"That's right, Brigadier. And I don't suppose Belton happened to mention to you that he was Melada's best mate?"

"He certainly did not. He never mentioned Melada, otherwise I might have suspected something."

"Like what?"

"I can't say exactly, but I would certainly have pricked my ears up if the first potential buyer had been mentioned by the second."

Masters got to his feet and moved over to stand by the window. As he peered out, he asked quietly: "Who paid for the notice? Melada?"

The Brigadier sounded regretful. "I'm afraid so. Our legal boys sent him a bill for twelve guineas. After all, he was the one who asked that they should do the job. Five for the notices and seven for posting."

"And Belton—or Heberden—had nothing to pay?"

"The luck of the draw. The law had been accommodated once. There was no need to repeat the gesture."

Masters turned. "I imagine Melada was pretty bitter about that extra blow?"

"He certainly didn't laugh when I told him. The only thing he didn't laugh at."

"Except, I imagine, the news that he had been outbid."

"That, of course."

"Of course. Now, sir, we came with the intention of borrowing the spare set of keys to the church."

"I wonder who borrowed the one from the pub at Oakby?"

"Heberden borrowed it from the landlord and hasn't returned it. And before you suggest we collect it from Heberden, you'd better know that he's gone missing, too."

The Brigadier screwed his eyes up in bewilderment.

"Missing? Heberden? What's going on in Oakby?"

"You tell us. But Heberden has not been seen or heard of for several days, and neither has the key."

The Brigadier got up and opened a cupboard. Hanging on cup hooks inside the door were a number of keys. He selected one and turned to hand it to Masters. "This is the only one held here. It is the vestry key—for the little door in the wall close to the well."

Masters thanked him and promised to return the key as soon as possible.

"That's the lot, I think," said Marchant. "There may have been small amounts of other drugs that I haven't mentioned, but as I say, speaking from memory and using the list of specialities as a prompt, that's the best I can do for you."

He was obviously wanting the three sergeants to leave so that he could get on with his business. This was so apparent that Iliff actually stood up ready to go, but Reed stayed seated. "A moment, please, sir. I'd like to annotate this list."

"What does that mean?"

"A lot of these things seem harmless enough to me. There's turpentine and linseed and ointments which I suppose wouldn't hurt a fly. But some of these medicines must be dangerous in the wrong hands. I'd like you to go through and mark those which have to be kept locked away."

"Oh, very well. Give it here."

"And...."

"And what?"

"I don't know much about veterinary medicine, sir, so I'd be pleased if you'd put me right on one point. Now I know that human medicines are often weight-related. You give a youngster half an aspirin for a headache whereas a fully grown woman will take two whole ones and a chap as big as myself needs three."

"What about it?"

"You treat animals of all sizes. From pet mice to carthorses and bulls, don't you?"

"Yes."

"Well, what I want to know is, do you ever use the same products for different sized animals?"

"Frequently."

"In that case, do you give a big animal a much bigger dose than a small animal? Or do you have different strengths of drugs?"

"Both."

"Would I be right in assuming that something which might be relatively harmless at ordinary strength might become dangerous at concentrated strength—even though basically it isn't classed as a dangerous drug?"

Marchant considered this for a moment and then grinned. "You're no fool, are you? The general answer is, of course, yes. Think about your own experience with, say, an antiseptic. Put a spoonful in a bowl of water and you can safely bathe a wound with it. Put it on neat and you could well burn away the tissue, to say nothing of hitting the ceiling in the process. But antiseptics, by and large, are not considered dangerous drugs even though, topical use aside...."

"Topical use?"

"External application. Leave that aside. If ingested they could cause all sorts of trouble—probably fatalities." Marchant was warming to his subject. Evidently he enjoyed airing his knowledge. "And when we come to medicine proper, if you read the list of contents, you'll often find that the active ingredient is as low as one per cent or less. So it follows that if pills, for instance, are compounded with an increased percentage of active ingredient they could well become dangerous, though not considered dangerous within the meaning of the Dangerous Drugs Act at their normal strengths."

Reed thanked him for the explanation and then added: "Would you be good enough to indicate not only the scheduled dangerous items, sir, but also those which are concentrated for use in large animals."

"Right. D for dangerous and F for concentrated."

"F for concentrated?" queried Iliff, as though he had not heard correctly.

"Jargon," replied Marchant without looking up from his list. "F for forte, meaning strong."

Iliff nodded his understanding and raised his eyebrows at Berger.

Webb was waiting for Masters and Green when they emerged from the office building after the interview with Alton.

"I didn't come in, Chief, in case I interrupted something."

"You missed a real good cup of chai," said Green. "Made with lemon."

"Don't care for it myself. Strong, milky and sweet's how I like it."

"Sugar," retorted Green, settling himself in the back seat. "Sugar, pure, white and deadly. That's what the quacks say."

"I saw you spooning sugar into coffee last night."

"That was brown," said Green. "And in any case, lad, do as I say, not as I do."

Webb turned to Masters.

"Melada's record, Chief."

"What about it?"

"He hasn't really got one."

"You mean the sky-pilot tried to bamboozle us?" asked Green.

"No."

"Either he has a record or he hasn't."

"Not in this country. He was jailed for fraud in Australia. Some shady deal he tried which didn't come off. If it had done it would have been considered a good business deal, but as it didn't, it was fraud. He was sentenced to three years, but after six months he was deported back to the U.K."

"We know of it, however."

"Yes, Chief. Of the deportation and the reasons for it, not the crime itself."

"Anything else?"

"Like the Reverend Canning said, he was put in front of the beaks for having cannabis in his house, but it didn't stick. Some smoker from the continent who visited him left a butt behind with traces in it. The locals evidently have long suspected Melada of shady behaviour, as he seemed to have no visible means of support, and when they got word that this continental was an addict, they went to Melada's house. But the bird had flown, leaving behind this butt, and they put Melada up for having the stuff on his premises."

"He got off, as the vicar said?"

"Just that, Chief, with the help of an expensive lawyer from London."

"Thanks. Now how's the time? What about killing half an hour or so in some tea shop and then we can call on Dr Watling in person, seeing we are in the city."

* * *

"Nothing," said Watling. "Not a sign anywhere in the body of what caused Belton's death."

"No marks or injuries?"

"I've been over his hide with a magnifying glass. Only on the back of his left hand is there a small graze. Not a hypodermic puncture or anything like that. Just a small mark such as one would find on any body at any time. Everybody knocks themselves, scratches themselves or makes some mark on the skin every day of their lives, usually without being aware of it."

"So you attach no importance to that mark on his hand?"

"None whatever."

"Would it help if you knew what you were looking for?"

"Not a scrap. Even if you could tell me exactly what caused the respiratory depression which led to his death, I couldn't find it, because there's nothing there to find. His organs and pathways are clear. So are his urine and bowel contents."

"So you can't suggest...."

"Not a hope, I'm afraid, Superintendent."

"But he was murdered."

"He was dead before he entered the water."

"That's good enough. And Melada?"

"Depressed fracture of the skull. That one was easy. I think he fell against a solid object with the result I've just mentioned. But I think he was pushed."

"Ah!"

"There were bruises about his face and chin, and the knuckle of his right hand bled for a very short time just before death."

"A punch-up?" asked Green.

"That is my interpretation of what I have found. The bruises were not fully formed before he died. After death, of course, they would not mature, but there were the beginnings of one or two beauties on his left cheek and chin and I think a shiner on his left eye. When I've finished I'll put it all in the report."

"Thanks. Were you present when the bodies were officially identified?"

"I was. Mrs Melada came in first. A slip of a thing with a drawl in her voice and spectacles that kept slipping to the end of her nose, no matter how often she pushed them back."

"Was she distressed?"

"Not visibly. There was emotion there. And although I shouldn't tell you this, because they were a wife's private words spoken over her husband's body and so, I believe, almost sacrosanct...."

"Almost? Was there a parson with her? Called Canning?"

"No. But because of the nature of this case, I'll tell you what she said. She merely looked at him and said quickly: 'Silly Johnny, I knew that church would bring disaster.' I took her words—as did the accompanying police officer—to mean positive identification of the body. But I got the impression she had sensed the coming of his death, and so there was no surprise at seeing his body. As I said, no visible distress, but an impression of well-controlled emotion."

"And Mrs Belton?"

"Different. Very different."

"Can you tell us?"

"Nothing factual. Only impressions. Mrs Belton was waiting outside in the little lobby until Mrs Melada had seen her husband's body. Identification of corpses by spouses, particularly, is not a pleasant experience and the police like to get it over with as quickly as possible. As Mrs Melada left, I was just behind her and witnessed the passing of the two women in the lobby."

"Passing?"

"I used the word advisedly, Mr Masters, because they did not meet. They passed. Now I heard that their menfolk were great friends. It doesn't follow that the women have to be bosom pals, too, but death is a great healer of rifts, should there be any in circumstances such as this. I paused, as did the policemen alongside Mrs Melada, expecting the two women to speak, if not to exchange a few words. She had been weeping and though somewhat more composed at the time, she patently did not want to see, acknowledge, or speak to Mrs Melada. Mrs Melada, on the other hand, looked hard at the woman. It would have been rather a severe stare in any case, because her glasses had again slipped to the end of her nose and so she was looking over them like a rather prim and disapproving school mistress. But there was more to it than that. As I said, I was slightly behind and to one side, so that when she turned her head towards Mrs Belton I got a good three-quarter profile view. Mr Masters, that glare was not benevolent."

"Not benevolent could be interpreted in several ways, doctor. Was it malevolent?"

Watling paused for a moment before replying, "On a man's face, yes, I would have described it as malevolent perhaps. But on a young woman's? Hatred? Disdain, maybe. A mixture of the two. It was momentary and I wasn't expecting it, but I can remember it was vivid enough to cause me to say to myself that there was no love lost between them. Quite honestly, I would almost have expected them to fall into each other's arms and weep in mutual grief. That would have been a natural thing to do with women who must have met each other socially on many occasions. But the link of sorrow was not there."

"Would you care to hazard a guess as to what might cause such enmity between them?"

"Not on your nelly. But there is a possibility that Mrs Melada in some way blamed Mrs Belton for Mr Melada's death."

"You would rule out a previous mutual dislike—during their husbands' lifetimes?"

"Not rule out. But as I've said, unless such a dislike were very deep-seated, I would have expected this double tragedy to draw them together, at least temporarily."

Masters nodded his understanding of Watling's point, thanked him and said goodnight. Green and Webb followed him out to the car.

"Bad blood among the women," said Green, "could mean anything or nothing—always supposing the doc wasn't mistaken about what he thought he saw."

"Meaning what?" asked Webb.

"Well," said Green, getting aboard the car and choosing a crumpled Kensitas very carefully from five or six, all in an equally disreputable state, "you weren't with us when we had our little chat with the Brigadier. Melada and Belton may have been all palsie-walsie, but Belton did Melada dirt over the business of the church."

"How?"

"Belton acted as agent for the bloke who outbid Melada."

"Who was that?"

"Heberden."

Webb drew away, whistling gently in surprise at this last piece of news. Masters turned to Green. "There are one or two questions we didn't put to Alton. We asked him if he had mentioned Melada to Belton, but we didn't ask if he'd mentioned Belton to Melada."

"Or Heberden to Melada."

"That, too. And there's a question of timing to be sorted out. Who died first? I've got the impression it was Melada. But am I right? Alton may be able to tell us which of them he saw last. That won't be proof, but it might help."

"Hold it, hold it!" said Green. "What if Belton died first? If he did, it's odds on that Melada was little Tommy Thin. He found out Belton had put the mockers on his deal and killed him in a fit of anger...."

"How?"

"Never mind how. He killed him and bunged him down the well. That got rid of one of the three who were implicated. That leaves two. Melada and Heberden. Heberden somehow gets to know that Melada has disposed of Belton—"

"A man like Heberden would have called us in," objected Webb.

"If he had time. Say he goes to the church expecting to meet Belton and finds Melada there instead. He is either told Belton is dead or he deduces it from what goes on.

109

Melada menaces him. Heberden realizes his own life is in danger. Melada threatens. Heberden defends himself with his stick...."

"What stick?" asked Webb. "I've heard nothing about Heberden carrying a stick."

"He was the local squire, wasn't he?" asked Green. "All local squires carry ash plants or shooting sticks. Badges of authority."

"I suppose we could check it out."

"Heberden is threatened. He defends himself. Gets home a few whacks and Melada stumbles backwards, cracking his crust on a gravestone. Before he knows where he is, Heberden finds he has a corpse on his hands. He's in a churchyard. The proper place for a corpse is a grave. He's not thinking straight. He decides to shove Melada under the sod...."

"He'd got a shovel handy, I suppose."

"No," replied Green. "But he knows where there is one."

"Where?"

"In the church. They used to have a coke house to store fuel for the stove...."

"You know that?"

"Everybody knows it. All churches used to have coke boilers or stoves. There was no electricity or gas at St John's—we know that—but I'll bet even the faithful didn't turn up to services in an unheated church. So there'd be a coke-heap, somewhere. And where there's a coke-heap, there's a shovel. And with everything being left in the church, nobody would remove a coke shovel. Heberden has the key. He lets himself in, grabs the shovel and starts to dig. He can't get very deep, because he's not a young man and in any case he'd need a spade to slice down very deep. So Melada goes in under nothing much more than the turves he'd had to lift. He feels safe, because he is in process of buying the property and when that happens he can stop anybody entering the churchyard, and nobody does visit the place anyhow."

"Then why has he run away?"

"Murder's a funny thing. I said he felt safe, but conscience raises doubts. Heberden remembers that there is one person who goes there—the vicar. A man who goes round looking for historical facts on gravestones. Then he'd buried the body near the hedge. Too near? Was there a gap? Would a passer-by notice a smell? These are the sorts of doubts he has. What is he to do? Make the classic mistake and return to the scene of the crime to put things right? Or is he to make off? He decides on the latter because it so happens that his wife is away and he's supposed to be going away from home himself. This is his golden opportunity. He'll get a week's start before he's missed. In a week he can be in Tahiti or Timbuctoo. So now he's been reported missing. But the police are not very keen on pulling all the stops out to find a mature man who is free to blow at any time if he wants to. So the hunt isn't even up yet."

Masters took his pipe from his mouth as Green came to the end of his reconstruction.

"It's got a lot going for it. I particularly liked the bits about the coke shovel and how events caused Heberden to take the course you attribute to him. But having said that—"

"You mean you didn't think of it, so you don't like it."

"What I was about to say was that though I hadn't thought about a theory in quite that light, having been, as I said, under the impression that Melada died first, I think we should keep what you have said in mind. But with a proviso. You said we shouldn't bother our heads at the moment as to how Belton died—or how Melada killed him. To my mind, that is central to your case. The bit about Heberden carrying an ash plant is immaterial. He could have picked up a piece of wood—a piece of a branch— to use as a weapon. That's a hurdle easily cleared, but not the way in which Melada disposed of Belton. We must know how that death came about before we can proceed with any theory—feasible though yours is."

Somewhat mollified, Green helped himself to another cigarette and said: "Why not ask one of the leading medical professors to list every cause of this what's-his-name? Respiratory depression? It could be that fright might cause it. If Melada threatened Belton, fear could cause him shock and shock might stop him breathing."

"Accidental death, you mean?"

"Sort of. Brought on by Melada's menacing attitude?"

"Then why tip him down the well? Melada would know he was in the clear. He hadn't laid a hand on Belton. Forensic would prove that. But he must have known that if he dropped him down a wellshaft on a property in which he, Melada, was known to be interested, questions would be asked as soon as the body was discovered."

"If it was discovered."

"The chances of discovery must have been high. Look how we came across it."

"Everybody isn't a nosey-parker from the Yard."

"But everybody looks down wells and drops stones down. Don't they, Mr Webb?"

"I always do," said Webb. "It's second nature. Always did it as a kid and the habit has stayed with me."

Green grunted to show he agreed and then lapsed into silence as the car ran into Market Rasen.

"Will you need me again tonight, Chief?" asked Webb.

"No, thank you. You get off. It's after seven o'clock. Unless you'd like a beer first?"

"I'd better not. The missus will be expecting me for supper."

"Lucky old toff!" said Green. "I'll bet this pub won't be producing anything up to the standard your old girl will put in front of you, judging by the looks of you. See you in the morning, laddie."

Masters and Green entered The Chestnut Tree to find Reed and Berger waiting for them.

"Shall I put the car away, Chief?" asked Reed.

Masters looked at Green. "It's a nice night. We'll have a talk over dinner and then, while the four of us are alone,

112

take a run in the country. We've never seen St John's and now I've got a key it might be interesting to take a peek inside."

"Suits me," said Green. "It'll keep these youngsters out of the bar."

"Who's talking?" asked Reed.

"I am," retorted Green, "and what I'm saying is, mine's a pint. I'll be sitting waiting over by the window when you've bought it."

The four of them sat only a short time in the bar before moving to the dining-room. Masters had asked Reed and Berger for a report and listened with approval while it was given.

"Here's the list, Chief," said Reed at the end.

Masters took it, and without looking at it, put it into his inside pocket. "I'd like to go over this later. I'd rather put you in the picture at this moment than speculate about a list—the names won't mean much to me anyway."

Masters left the report largely to Green who, with elephantine memory, had near-total recall. By the time they rose from dinner, Reed and Berger knew as much about the case as the other two.

"We haven't seen the three women yet," said Green as they made their way to the car. "We're leaving it a bit late, aren't we?"

Masters agreed. "It was my intention to see them today. I'm very conscious of the fact that we ought to have interviewed them at the outset, but events have led us astray. I know we shouldn't let them divert us, but I'm not unhappy with what we've got today."

"I should hope not." Green took his nearside rear seat and Masters got in beside him. "Last night at this time we hadn't a clue."

"True. And I'm consoling myself with the thought that knowing what we now know, our interviews with the three wives will be that much more penetrating. For instance, if Reed gets those lenses measured tomorrow...."

"Measured, chief?"

"Yes. Take them to an optician. He'll have a little wheel-like gadget on the end of an arm leading from a central spindle. He centres the spindle and twists the arm and the wheel somehow measures the focal length of the eye-piece. They can even do it with half a lens. They have to be able to in case where some patient comes in with broken glasses for which they have no record. They measure the previous lenses to get a starting point for the new test."

"What's it going to do for us, Chief?"

"Maybe nothing. But it could mean we'd know what sort of eyesight the fire-raiser has. People don't usually travel far from home for specs, do they? And there can't be that many oculists locally."

"What if they're not his spectacles, Chief?"

"I won't say they've got to be, but how do you get hold of at least two pairs of other people's glasses?"

"Easy," grunted Green. "You just pick 'em up. People always leave them lying around and they're not the sort of articles you expect to be pinched, so...." He shrugged. "But we should do it, all the same. Just in case."

Masters nodded. "Then we ask the wives the names of their opticians. We know Happy Melada wears glasses and it's likely Mrs Heberden and her husband do—being middle-aged. Whether Mrs Belton does or her husband did we shall have to discover. You never know your luck. Something could come up."

The car drew up at the church gate. The young constable on duty was sitting on the top bar with his heels hooked into a lower one. He didn't get down to begin with—presumably thinking this was a rubber-necking party—but after Reed had had a brief word with him he was on his feet very smartly.

"Any callers, constable?"

"Not since I've been on, sir. The party searching the churchyard had gone before that."

"Thank you. But don't stay at the gate all the time. Move about to keep an eye on the hedges."

"Right, sir."

Masters led the way up to the south door and then swung right along the overgrown path. He rounded the east end and the well, with a barrier of white tape round it, was before them. In the wall of the church, up two small steps, was the vestry door. Masters opened it. It swung back over a step just big enough to take it, and then followed two more small steps.

"This is a death trap," complained Green. "Fancy trying to find your way in here for choir practice on a dark night without a light."

They stood in the small robing vestry with its hanging cupboards and two bench seats. Opposite the entrance was another door into the chancel at the altar stairs. To the left a third door led down two steps into the vicar's vestry. Here were more cupboards, a rusting old safe, a variety of chairs and a table under a leaded window.

"There's a double door here," said Reed, from the end of the robing vestry opposite the vicar's vestry. They were more lightly built than the other doors, and when opened, revealed two steps down into the church proper.

"There for the choir to get in and out," said Masters. "I suppose they sometimes filed in singing the Introit and out singing the Recessional."

"We've all been to church," said Green. "We know the difference between matins and evensong."

"I'm sure you do. But I was not aware you knew the form behind the scene. But I won't bother with explaining the piscina and—"

"The what? Oh, come on." He stumped down the steps.

"No smell of damp," said Berger, sniffing the air.

"It's musty."

"That's dust. Dry dust. Not mildew."

They stood and took stock of the furnishings which had been left in the little church. The evening sun streamed in to gild certain pieces and to throw dark shadows. It seemed as though St. John's had just been locked up after one particular service and never opened again until they had come in. The pews were still there, and the font. Even the lectern, with two purple bookmarks. The Bible had gone, as had all the consecrated pieces. Altar frontals, communion plate, crucifix and wardens' staves—many such things had been removed, but Masters could appreciate that a lot of valuable material still remained and he guessed that this had not escaped Melada. In fact, Masters guessed, the contents still left were probably worth more in the open market than the two thousand Melada had bid for the property and contents.

In the main body of the church were just seven pews on each side of the centre aisle. Behind the cross-aisle leading from the south door were two more on each side of the tongue-shaped stone step which carried the font and led to the ringing chamber at the base of the tower.

The choir stalls were there, the altar rail and a prie-dieu.

"The timber here," said Green, "is worth a fortune. Solid oak."

"What if one were to sell the pews separately?"

"The Americans would pay a bomb. A bench from a cute little church in Lincoln Shire for a house porch in Texas! To sit on and chew a corn cob!"

Masters led the way round the pulpit, and up the chancel steps. As he arrived at the altar steps, he said to Green: "I've a hankering to see that empty tomb."

Green shrugged. He followed Masters towards the altar table. The slabs were in shadow, but it was easy to see how well they had been cut. They fitted each other and their ledge exactly.

"They're all in place," said Green. "You'd be lucky to get a penknife between them. So how are you going to lift one?"

Masters knelt for a closer look and to run his fingers over the joins, appreciating the accuracy of the work. He suddenly stopped his hands and went back a bit with his fingers. "There's an inequality here."

"You don't say!"

"Not a sharp bump, a rounded one. Here, Reed, strike a match and hold it down here, would you."

Reed did as he was asked. Masters found the place and scratched it with his fingernail.

"It's transparent, Chief," said Reed. "It's glue. Glue that's been squeezed up by the stones."

Masters didn't reply. He took a small penknife from his pocket and, concentrating on his task, while Reed continued to light matches, shaved the protuberance away very slowly and carefully. At last he had it. He put it on his palm to exhibit it—a piece of greyish, translucent dried varnish or resin, barely half an inch long and a sixteenth of an inch deep, the top rounded by the natural settling flow of the glue as it dried.

"The laddo's right," said Green. "Any more of it down there?"

"At a guess," said Masters, getting to his feet, "it's on all four edges of the slabs."

"You mean somebody has sealed the tomb with glue?"

"With epoxyresin, using it as an adhesive and a sealant."

"Why?" asked Berger.

"Why?" echoed Green. "As an adhesive to hold those stones down so that nobody could lift one without going to great trouble—seeing there's no handhold and they fit like a glove. And as a sealant to keep in the stink."

"The stink?"

"Of death, boy. Death."

"Go to the car, Reed, and fetch the torch," said Masters quietly. "Bring the entrenching tool, too. The pick end might help. Get the constable to call up. I want a message sent to Mr Webb. I want stone-cutting tools here immediately. Got that?"

"Yes, Chief."

"Go with him, Berger. You can bring the implements while he's getting the message through."

When the two sergeants had gone, Masters turned to Green. "I think this will put an end to your theory."

Green nodded and, despite the fact that he was in church,

117

took out his cigarette packet.

He had smoked three Kensitas, while Reed and Berger had failed to raise a slab, before Webb arrived. Masters had been insistent that the stonework should not be broken and, without this, nowhere was there a gap wide enough to take the entrenching tool.

Webb came in first, alone, dressed in slacks and a sweat shirt.

"What did your missus give you for dinner, Webby?"

Webb stared at Green, astounded. "You didn't ask me out here to..."

"No lad. Just being friendly. What did she give you?"

"Beef pie and Brown Becky."

"What did I tell you! And I had to do with something called blanket of lamb."

"Did you fetch a stone-cutting tool, Mr. Webb?"

"Yes, Chief. It's coming in. A petrol-driven job. Like a treefeller really, but with one of those cutting discs attached. What's it wanted for?"

"You heard the vicar describe the empty tomb?"

"Under the altar?"

"The slabs have been sealed down."

"Cement?"

"Epoxyresin. We can't get at them to lift one. Your machine should be able quite easily to cut along one of the sealed joins, widening it enough for us to get a lever in."

Webb said: "Who'd want to seal that?"

"More to the point, why?"

Webb looked startled. "I was wondering...?"

"Why we want to see inside the tomb?"

"Yes."

"Why do you think it's been sealed?"

"Heberden?"

"We shall soon know."

"After all," said Green, "it was built as a vault for his family."

Whoever had set the stones in the epoxyresin had done a thorough job. The under-surfaces, where they were in contact with the ledges, as well as all the edges of each slab, had been liberally coated. The strength of the glue and the lack of leverage space had made the job perfect. The young country policeman who used the stone cutter had to spend a long time on the first slab before it could eventually be levered out. Even then it was only done by sawing through the glue bond on all four sides, down to the ledge. Gradually, after much levering, with Reed using his feet to get some power on the entrenching tool, the slab began to move a little. At last it was up. There was no need to ask what was inside. The stench that rose from the hole even before Berger had lifted the slab clear told its own tale. Green, Masters and Webb peered in, with the torch giving them light to do so. A man's figure in slacks and shirt, with no jacket.

"Heberden?" asked Masters, seeing the close-cropped grey hair, the neat moustache and the still well-set collar and tie.

"You knew?" asked Webb.

"Come along, Webby," said Green. "Let the lads get the other slabs up while you tell me what Brown Becky is."

— 6 —

Watling arrived before the ambulance. He stood alongside Masters while the police photographers took their pictures and then stepped across to the tomb. "I don't think I can roll him over in there," he said. "Damn difficult to get at in fact, because there's no room for me to get in with him."

Green said: "And aren't you pleased about that, doc!"

"Not really. He's not in too bad a shape, you know. Probably the sealing has helped delay putrefaction." He knelt beside the tomb, considering the situation for a few moments. Then: "I think we'll have him out, and that's not going to be too easy." He turned to the kit he had brought in with him, and from a sealed plastic bag, took a neatly folded bundle of plastic sheeting. "We can't get the other side of him and these damned arches are in the way in front, so we'll have to tackle it from the ends." He turned to Masters. "That must have been the way he was fed in, you know. No other way possible."

Masters nodded. "What would you like us to do?"

"I want to put this sheet under him and then lift him out. I propose to start from the feet. Now, if your sergeants would put the two slabs back in position at the head end, I could get under the table and lie on them. I can lift his feet and you can then slip the end of the sheet under the backs of his legs, probably up as far as his b.t.m. Then I can come back and we could probably draw him on to the sheet by pulling gently on his legs. Anyhow, let's try."

Reed and Berger replaced two of the flags. Watling crept on all fours under the north-end arch of the table and lay on his stomach on the replaced stones, with his upper half over the still open portion of the tomb. Masters knelt at the southern end, with the plastic sheet pushed up into a long bundle across his knees.

"Ready?" asked Watling.

"Yes."

Green directed the torch downwards so that Watling could see to get his hands under the trousered legs of the corpse. He grasped just above the ankles and lifted. The shoes came above the lip of the tomb and the roll of plastic went under the heels. "Keep them up," said Masters. "I'm pulling the whole lot under. Then I'll draw out this end."

It was difficult work, yet it went extremely well. Reed had to pin the roll down with the entrenching tool so that Masters did not pull the whole sheet out again. But they managed it. If anything the other end was easier because the legs now held the sheet, and once the upper part of Heberden's body was raised, the roll came out with no impediment.

"Central lift," warned Watling when the slabs had once more been removed. "Bring both sides of the shroud together on top." Reed and Berger did as they were told. "Fine. Now we'll take him out head first. Easy does it. Lift!"

The body was heavy and the sergeants were kneeling outside the arches and lifting inside. There was no straight lift, only a straining of arms and shoulders as they sought to move the corpse in two directions at once—upwards and longitudinally. Masters helped by kneeling close by the shoulders of the dead man and, as soon as there was room, by inserting the spade portion of the stout little entrenching tool below the body. He was able to exert some leverage: enough to tip the balance in favour of the sergeants. Reed, with Watling's help, manoeuvred Heberden's shoulders through the arch. After that it was plain sailing. The shrouded bundle was lifted carefully and placed in the chancel between the choir stalls.

"I'll just take a quick look," said Watling, squatting to open the plastic. His expert hands felt the back of the skull, the ribs and long bones for fractures and he examined the face and neck for contusions. As he finished he got to his feet. "No visible signs of injury."

"Meaning what?" asked Masters.

"That we could have another Belton on our hands."

"Respiratory depression," said Green resignedly.

"That's it."

"I'd like to know as soon as possible, doctor. With three corpses on my hands and no explanation as to how they died or came to be disposed of in the places where we've found them, I think it behoves us to get an answer at the earliest possible moment."

"Quite right, Superintendent. When this gets out, people will begin to panic. They'll think there's a madman loose, and they'll be quite right. I'm beginning to feel spooky about this place myself. And for heaven's sake check the church tower and every other nook and cranny round here in case there are any more victims about."

Masters smiled. "My guess is we've unearthed the lot."

"I'm pleased to hear you say so. Not that I think you've been wasting much time in the past twenty-four hours. What you've achieved is almost unbelievable."

"The job isn't really begun yet, doctor. It only starts with the finding of the body."

"True. Now, everybody, wash your hands. The ambulance driver has brought in a bucket of water strongly laced with benzalkonium chloride. There's carbolic soap and paper towels. Give yourselves a good scrub-up."

Masters had his jacket off and his sleeves rolled up and was soaping himself thoroughly when Watling, similarly engaged, said: "I'll work all night if necessary on this one, Superintendent."

"Thank you. Is there any way in which my team can help?"

"No. You've got enough on your plate already. Have a good night's kip and ring me at nine in the morning. If I'm not at the lab, give me a call at home. Webb knows the numbers."

"I'm grateful."

"There's no need to be. You're doing a good job for us. I'm doing mine. Don't forget that I am, in reality, part of your team for this little show. You've set me a puzzle, and a challenge. I don't intend to let either beat me."

Because they were guests at The Chestnut Tree, they were entitled to drink even though the bar was closed, and because they were who they were, the manager made no demur at serving them after hours.

Webb had gone to inform Mrs Heberden that her husband had been found dead. Masters had cautioned him to say no more than that. Simply to state that her husband had died—apparently of natural causes—in the church, and that she would, in due course, be asked to identify the body.

So there were the four of them sitting in the otherwise deserted lounge. Green said, after the manager had served their beer, "I don't know whether any of you noticed, but I felt in his pockets for the church key. Not that I expected to find it, but I thought I'd better confirm it wasn't there. And it wasn't on the inside of the south door lock, either."

"Thanks," said Masters. "It was the right thing to do, even though the chances of it being found inside the church are a million to one against. For no matter what Watling finds—or does not find—as the cause of death, we know Heberden was certainly not capable of sealing himself in his ancestor's tomb. That must mean, in my view, that he, like Belton, was somehow murdered and that the murderer would need the key to let himself out of the building and to lock up behind him. So the key could be anywhere. That being so, apart from the precautionary search the DCI made, I don't propose to waste time searching for it further."

There was a murmur of agreement from his three listeners and then Green spoke again. "You half-expected to find Heberden there," he accused. "All that rubbish about going for a run in the country to have a look round the church. You headed for that altar like a long-dog as soon as you decently could. And don't deny it, because otherwise you wouldn't have run your fingers over those cracks and found that glue. I've known you long enough to know that the moment you felt it you started to gloat. Unless you'd expected something, a little bump like that dab of glue would have meant nothing."

Reed asked: "What are you getting het up about? If the Chief had a hunch and it proved to be right, that's a cause for congratulation, not for slanging him."

"Watch it, laddo," cautioned Green.

"I agree with him," added Berger.

Masters sat back to listen.

"What I was going on about," said Green, "was not the fact that he guessed the body was there and then found it."

"It sounded to me as if it was."

"Because you don't listen, chum. It was the fact that His Nibs had guessed...."

"And guessed right."

"As it turned out. But he couldn't tell us beforehand, could he? Oh, no! He had to pretend he just wanted to look inside the church. And for why? Because if his guess hadn't been right, he would have looked a fool. That's all I'm saying. He pitched us a yarn just so's it didn't look as though he'd made a bloomer."

"What's wrong in that? If he'd said to you at dinner time that he reckoned Heberden's body was in that tomb, you'd have laughed at him."

"Who says I would?"

"I do. Because that's your form."

"All right. Maybe I would, if he'd just said it out of the blue. But not if he'd explained: made out a good case why he thought so."

"Perhaps you're right," Masters said to Green. "I ought to have had enough confidence in my own theory to have taken you into my confidence. But we did mention that Heberden might be there earlier, if you remember, and I assure you it was not because I thought you would scoff if I started a wild goose chase."

"No? What was it then?"

"It was because it was too easy."

"It couldn't have been," said Reed. "None of us got it. If it had been so easy we'd have all been on to it."

"Easy once you got on to the right track. Three men missing. All three lives interlinked by the church. Two of them found at the church. Where would you expect the third to be? At the church. Whereabouts at the church, bearing in mind one of those found was in a grave and one down a well? The church is locked and the key missing. Could the third be in the church itself? Our murderer likes variety in his choice of graves. What variety would he find inside the church? No less than a ready-made tomb, empty and get-at-able. And then to cap it all, the missing man is called Heberden and the tomb was built specifically for a man called Heberden." He paused for a moment. "Somehow it seemed, as I said, so easy, that I had my doubts. So you see, I didn't know. If the body hadn't been there, I'd have known it was too good to be true. In fact, that it was there was a surprise. Maybe I seemed to gloat. I don't think I did. I was surprised. Pleasantly surprised. And I have not yet said a word to show I thought I was pulling off some smart coup." He faced Green. "So if you think I was jammy, which in the past is an expression you've often used about me, I plead guilty, but I prefer to call it lucky."

Green had listened attentively. When Masters had finished, he said: "You know, marriage has done you good. I always said that your little missus was a cracker, now I'm even more convinced. For anybody to change you to the point where you'd make a speech like that is a miracle. Next time my good lady and myself visit you I shall tell her so."

Masters laughed aloud. "She'll tell you different. But Wanda is a remarkable girl. After all, Greeny, she's always thought a hell of a lot of you, and that's saying something."

Green reddened. "We have a very special relationship, me and Wanda. She relies on me for hints as to how to manage you. That's why she's making such a good job of being your wife. And if you tell me you weren't jammy

125

to get her, I'll clout you, big as you are."

Reed asked quietly: "Can anybody join in this domestic quarrel? Or do we just forget we've got three murders on our hands?"

Green glowered at him. "Was there something special you wanted to say, lad? Like asking if anybody might want one of your fags?"

Reed threw his packet on the table and said: "Yes, there was. It's the murderer."

"What about him?"

"Motive. What motive could he have? It looks as if that church itself is the reason for all three deaths. But why? If the murderer is so keen on a redundant church that he is prepared to kill off everybody who attempts to buy it, does he do it to preserve some secret connected with it?"

"You mean is there something about the church—something sinister or illegal—that we haven't unearthed yet?"

"Yes. That's what I mean. Unless somebody is going to tell the murders are motiveless."

"Are you asking for a definite answer or an opinion?" asked Masters.

"Either, Chief."

"Then I will give it as my opinion that the murders were not motiveless."

"And that," sneered Green, "is as safe a bet as saying that a pig can't fly."

"Perhaps," agreed Reed. "But at any rate I'm satisfied."

"That there is something odd about the church?"

"Yes. It's a sort of...what's the word?...lodestone. It's got to be."

"And what do you suggest we do about it?"

"Find out who has a particular interest in the church."

"I can tell you one."

"Who?"

"The Reverend William Canning." Green said it with relish. "Shall we go out and arrest him?"

But the tone did not rile Reed. He replied: "Well, he knew all about the proposed purchase; he goes there to inspect gravestones; he knows the history of Heberden's tomb; he's a strongly built, youngish man, capable of the physical acts necessary to topple bodies into wells and vaults; it could be that his faith is so fanatical that he won't permit a former sacred building to be turned over to secular purposes; it could be that there's something in that votive thing he mentioned which cuts off half his stipend if and when St John's falls into disrepair or is burned down or ceases to be a place of worship for any reason."

"Okay, okay! You've made your point."

"Very well," added Masters. "We can't ignore Canning."

"Too many ifs and buts," grunted Green.

"Agreed, but there are further points to Reed's case. Canning would be accepted by Melada and by Heberden. They wouldn't be wary of him if he suddenly joined them at the church. We don't know whether he was known to Belton, but I don't believe many people would be suspicious of a parson. So he would disarm them."

"You'll be saying next," said Green, "that the mysterious cause of their respiratory depression was some incantation by the skypilot. A sort of witch doctor's curse."

"Well...." began Masters.

"Oh, no!" groaned Green. "Not the occult."

"Nothing like that. I was merely about to observe that most people would begin to think there was a curse on a building that had claimed three victims."

"That's a thought," said Reed. "Like that big diamond that brings tragedy to whoever owns it."

"Hope," said Green.

"I am doing," replied Reed. "Hoping that we can get a line on whoever's killing off the local populace. Then we can go home."

Masters got to his feet. "Bed," he said. "We're beginning to maunder."

"That's a word to go to bed with," grumbled Green.

Masters rang Watling promptly at nine from Webb's office.

The pathologist was still in his lab and sounded thoroughly tired and dispirited.

"Not a sausage, Superintendent. Heberden died in exactly the same way as Belton."

"Respiratory depression?"

"That's it. But I can find no cause. Of course, he's an older man, but he was in good shape, and my examination—a very thorough examination—has shown no reason why he should have died in this way."

"No marks on the body?"

"Nothing of any importance. As I told you, everybody has the odd minor graze or bruise at any given moment. I've never yet examined a body that didn't have some mark caused by bumping into furniture, or by gardening or scratching an itching part or some such thing. Heberden is no different. He's got a gnat bite on his hairline, a graze on his forearm due, I would guess, to pruning roses, and a red pressure mark on his right foot. But none of them is significant. They are in no way serious."

"So no hypodermic marks and no signs of ingestion of some toxic substance?"

"None whatever. And that is puzzling me. So just in case I've gone gaga, I'm having a colleague of mine go over the bodies."

"Repeating your work?"

"No. Starting from scratch in his own way. So as not to inhibit him at all, I'm leaving the lab now. I only stayed on to take your call. Now I'm going home for some sleep."

"When will I know the results of your colleague's investigations?"

"I'll be back here at five this afternoon."

"May I ring you then?"

"Please do. And believe me I'm as anxious as you are to clear this up. I don't like being beaten as completely as this."

Green who had been standing by and had gathered the gist of the conversation, grimaced. "How the hell can we be expected to wrap up a case when forensic can't even tell us what killed them? It's working in the dark."

Webb, who was with them, said: "The fact that there are three bodies makes it bad enough. When you've got a job to find out what killed them before you start on who killed them makes it well-nigh impossible to my mind. I'm glad we've got you lot here to deal with it, because we certainly couldn't."

Masters started to pack the first pipe of the day. "It's pretty bad," he admitted, "but not hopeless. We know how Melada was killed—not who killed him—but how he was killed. That could mean that we've got a foot in the door." He looked across at Green. "As that seems to be the most likely way of entering, I suggest we concentrate on that for now."

"At least it tells us which of these three women we should see first."

"Happy Melada. I'm anxious to meet her."

Webb said: "Do you need me, Chief? I've got a few other things to do if you can find your own way about the patch now."

"Right you are, Mr Webb. We'll call on you if we need you."

The house was isolated. To get to it, Reed, who was driving, had to turn off the main road and travel two hundred yards down a track which had at one time been dressed with road metal which had prevented it from becoming nothing more than a rutted way. But there was no top dressing on the stones, and it was a fair guess that had the volume of traffic been anything other than very light, the lane would have been a morass in winter.

The car stopped at a five-barred gate on which was a highly-coloured hand-painted board reminiscent of an inn sign. 'John and Happy's Shack' it read. 'Open all hours.' The illustration was of a castle embodying some of the features of Windsor.

"Some shack," said Berger as he got down to open the gate. "Somebody has a sense of humour."

"Had," corrected Masters. "We saw some of Melada's sketches yesterday afternoon. He wasn't a bad draughtsman."

The track continued across a small field which was, apparently, the Shack's garden. Two or three small areas had been cultivated and there were some good-looking crops of vegetables and flowers. Then came a belt of poplars in full leaf and behind them the house. It was of wood, white-painted, and two-storied.

"Tucked well away," said Green, opening his door and stepping down. As he did so, the front door of the house opened and a little Yorkshire terrier shot towards them, yapping shrilly. It went for Green's trouser legs, darting in to attack and away again before he could lay hands on it.

"Berger," he roared. "Get this clockwork mouse off me."

"He's taken a fancy to you," said Berger, coming round to try to pick up the animal. But even he could not catch it, and the game was only over when a nasal voice called: "Goliath! Come here! Goliath!"

The dog stopped, half-crouched for another run at Green, turned its head and then sped off towards the door. Then it leapt, and landed safely in the arms of the young woman standing there.

"Goliath!" muttered Green.

"Of Gath!" murmured Masters as he passed him on the way to the porch.

"With hith helmet of bwath," added Reed and followed Masters.

"We're policemen," said Masters. "Are you Mrs Melada?"

Happy held Goliath in one arm and pushed her glasses back on her nose. She was just as Canning had described her.

"Not actually," she said. "But I lived with him."

"I see. What would you like me to call you?"

"Happy will do."

"And I shall be happy to comply. I expect you know why we're here."

130

"Are you the Scotland Yard men who found John?"

"Yes. May we come in?"

She nodded and turned into the house, leading the way into a large living-room out of which ran the stairs. "I can't put Goliath down," she drawled, "because there are no doors on any of our rooms, so I can't shut him away."

"Not on any room?" asked Green. "Not even the...er ...bathroom?"

"Nope."

She gestured to them to sit where they could and they took their choice from a selection of chairs and sofas which, Masters guessed, had been bought at auction sales over the years.

"Now, Happy, Mr John Melada's death must be a great blow to you," said Masters. "May I, at the onset, say how sorry we are about it and at having to be here."

"I guess I've got over the worst of it."

"But his body was only discovered yesterday."

"I've known for a long time that he was dead. A fortnight at least." She said it without apparent emotion. The four men were silent for a moment, watching her carefully as the little terrier, sensing the tension, put up his muzzle to lick his mistress's face.

"Known?" said Masters at last. "Not suspected or feared?"

"You're out for precision, Mr Masters. You've got it. I said known and I meant known."

"I'll accept your word, Miss Happy, but you must realise your reply prompts me to ask how you came to know."

"I worked it out."

"I see. You weren't present at his death?"

"No. I worked it out."

"And you didn't know where his body was?"

"I still don't know, exactly."

"You what?" asked Green. "You mean to say they didn't tell you when they took you to identify him?"

"They said near to St John the Divine's church in Oakby. That's not very precise, is it?"

Masters was marvelling at her composure.

131

"Until you had identified Mr Melada's body there was no point in giving you the details. But afterwards? Didn't you ask?"

"The constable who drove me back here had no details."

"I see. Your husband was buried in the churchyard."

"Buried?"

"Does that surprise you?"

"No. I ought to have guessed it."

"How could you have guessed it?"

"Because I went there to look for him and couldn't find him."

Green held up his hand. "Wait a moment, Miss. You say you went there to look for him. When?"

"After he went missing."

"After you knew he was dead? After you'd worked it out?"

"That's right."

Green glanced at Masters to convey that he'd never met anything quite like this before and he wasn't quite sure how to proceed. Masters, however, was prepared to tackle the situation. "Miss Happy, for you to work out that your husband was dead, you would need some solid fact on which to build. I suppose, too, that intuition came into it?"

"A little. If you can call a woman's knowledge of her man intuition."

"May we know the processes and the premises which enabled you to reach the conclusion which was verified as correct yesterday when the body was found?"

"Sure. Why not?"

"Please tell us."

"You knew Johnny was set on buying that old church?"

"We knew that much."

"But did you know how set on it he was?"

"Obviously not the degree of his...."

"Obsession would be the right word."

"Please explain."

"I don't think I can. As you can guess, I've thought about it a lot. Suddenly, one day, we see a church for sale. I

132

guess the word church had never crossed Johnny's lips, let alone entered his mind, for ten years. And yet on that day he became obsessed with the idea of owning it."

"As a business venture perhaps."

"Perhaps. It had everything going for it as far as Johnny was concerned. Things to do—design, decorate, furnish, install heat, light and water, clear the graveyard. An endless list of things he could have used up his energy on. He wanted that. He wanted something of his own for the first time in his life."

"Surely, this house...."

"Is rented. Johnny wanted a stake. But it couldn't be an ordinary house. It had to be a monument. Something that had stood for years and just waiting for him to put the finishing touches to: something that was unique and different from anything anybody else had. Johnny had to be different, that's why we've got no doors here, not even on the loo."

"The church would not have made as nice a home as this house."

"It wasn't to be a home. It was to be a studio to be let to artists of various sorts."

"Simply that? No other plans for it?"

"I guess not. I accused Johnny of wanting to turn it into a porn shop. He was capable of just that. It would have appealed to his sense of humour. I still reckon I was right. But he denied it and nobody can prove what he would have done now. So let's just say he's got this obsession."

"And what did you feel about the place?"

She pushed her glasses up her nose and stared straight at Masters. "It scared the pants off me. I walked round that deserted graveyard and I found it spooky. In broad daylight. I was there for half an hour on my own and I didn't like it."

"So you tried to dissuade Mr Melada from buying it."

"Yeah. But Johnny was a clever old cuss. He told me I could fix the price he offered."

"That sounds reasonable."

"Not if you don't want to lose a guy who's obsessed by

133

a church, it's not. Fix it too low an' he'll have you for causing him to lose it. Fix it too high and you're a pauper enjoying love on a shoestring, and I don't think."

"Difficult for you. What did you do?"

"Did the only thing possible with obsessionists. I fixed it at the maximum possible consistent with keeping out of the poor house and gave him the reasons for what I'd done so as he'd know how I'd arrived at it."

"Was he satisfied?"

"Not satisfied. But it was what he offered."

"May we know about it? Your proposals and his reactions at the time?"

"Why?"

Green said: "Look, lass, your old man got clobbered. We want to know what went on. You ask the Superintendent why. And the answer to that is a lemon. We suck it and see. A lot of what we hear is of no use to us. But we don't know that until after we've heard it. So come on. When did you explain to John Melada how you'd decided what he could pay for the church?"

"The next morning. The day after we'd seen the church."

"It must have been early. He went to see Brigadier Alton that morning."

"Yeah! It was at breakfast time."

"What were you eating?"

"Me? Muesli, like I always do."

"And Johnny?"

"He was eating a plate of cold stew left over from the night before."

"For breakfast?" asked Berger in disbelief. "Cold stew?"

Happy looked solemnly—over her glasses—at the young sergeant.

"It's not to everybody's taste, but he liked it."

"Just watching him eat it would be enough for me."

"I didn't watch him. I was reading the *Guardian*."

Green came in again. "Did he ask you what you'd decided?"

"Yeah. He said, well? and I asked, well what? and he said, the price I can pay, and I said two thousand pounds."

"What did he do then?"

"What he always did. He laughed and said he couldn't get a cowshed for that and I was expecting him to offer it for the church and two acres of ground. So I asked him what value was two acres full of graves and he said, come on, Happy, how did you get that figure."

"And?"

"I told him that two thousand was the amount mentioned by the vicar and he said to hell with that because it only went to show that the church would be cheap but not that cheap."

"What did you say to that?"

"That I had worked at it. I'd added up what I reckoned he'd get for the internal furnishings—the pews and things—and doubled it. He asked if I thought that the fabric and land were only worth the same amount as the pews but I didn't answer that one. I told him I'd looked at our savings and that between us we might just raise two thousand if we emptied my Building Society book and cashed our National Savings."

"He accepted you'd done your best?"

"I told him I hadn't tried to limit him in any way as I'd given him everything we'd got. He made some snide comment to the effect that everything we'd got just happened to coincide with the figure the vicar had mentioned and the figure I'd worked out before I'd added up our assets."

"He had a point."

"He made it. I told him it was fate and he said he couldn't accept that. So I said, lover, if you really want to know the value I put on that church it was nothing, zero, rien, sweet-fanny but, seeing we can scrape up two thousand...and I left it at that."

"He was satisfied at last?"

"It's obvious you didn't know Johnny. He said, OK, two thousand as a deposit it is, and I said two thousand top price, deposit ten per cent of that. Then he said oh, come on, Hap, when I said you could fix the price I expected you to be realistic. So I read him a lecture. I told him people shouldn't buy what they don't need if they can't afford it. And we didn't need a church and couldn't afford more than two thousand, so that was that."

"And that was the end of it?" Green was at his best. Masters had left it to him, and he was determined to show his colleagues how such interrogations should be conducted.

"Johnny started to talk about it being an investment and I asked him if he got the church for two thousand what return would we get on it. He said, as it stands, nothing. But after it was done up, a lot. So I asked how much would doing up a church cost and after a bit of argument he agreed that the church itself would cost another two thousand and to clear the churchyard and dig a septic tank another thousand."

"Five thousand in all."

"That's right, and I told Johnny it seemed a low figure but asked him what he'd get as a holiday home. He went on about it being a studio or a place for groups to rehearse and I said he wouldn't be able to let a stone-cold church in that place in winter. In the summer months, perhaps, I told him. Say twenty weeks a year at—if he was lucky—an average of forty pounds a week. He said average fifty, so I accepted that and told him he'd gross a thousand a year, of which about three hundred and fifty would be tax. Of course he said he didn't pay tax and usually he didn't. But this wouldn't have been one of his private little cash deals. He'd have to advertise for custom and people would want receipts. And there'd be rates and maintenance. So I reckoned he wouldn't make more than four hundred a year on an investment of five thousand, to say nothing of the work he'd have to put in. I told him it would take thirteen or fourteen years to get his money back and he'd make more by putting it into a building society to compound—if he'd got it to put in, that is."

"That wasn't the end of the matter, I'll bet. If I've got your Johnny right, he'd say he could raise the three thousand somehow."

"You're right. He did. So I asked what we were arguing about. He could still bid two thousand for the church. He

136

laughed and said he wouldn't get it for that and I said that was what I was counting on because even at that price he'd be in deep water and if he went any higher he'd be in dead trouble. So he said it was obvious I didn't want him to have it and I said I'd never disguised that fact but I'd kept my promise and fixed the price.

"Knowing it won't be accepted, he said, so I asked him straight out why he was so dead-set on acquiring an empty old church in the middle of nowhere and he asked why I was so keen to stop him."

"Why were you?" asked Green.

"I told him I didn't want to buy trouble, but he didn't answer my question. He just said he wanted it, again and again."

"But you knew different?"

"I reckon—as I told you—he'd got an idea to set it up as a studio all right—a film studio for blue films, and a center—a porn center. I reckon he thought people—kinky people—would pay big money for the kick of having sex in a church and I know he was keen to break into the porn book market."

"Did you tell him this is what you thought?"

"Yes."

"What did he say?"

"He laughed and said it would rake in the bread. So I told him not to be daft because we knew the police had their eye on him ever since he got off that drugs charge. And besides, I wasn't for getting into that sort of thing."

"Was that it?"

"More or less. He still said he wanted it just for a studio and I told him I was frightened of that church, I was frightened by the deal, and I was frightened by what he was going to do. And that's why I said he could have everything we'd got, but not a penny more. He said I knew he wouldn't get the church for that and I said, that's right, you won't get a cowshed for that price."

Green sat back. "Thanks, love. That was very clear. Would you like a fag?"

She shook her head and then looked down at Goliath

who was simulating sleep in her arms. Masters said gently: "But Mr Melada nearly did get his church."

"Yeah! He was so confident, he came home and told me he had got it. He was like a dog with two tails for the next fortnight while he waited to hear, and when he saw those notices posted he was sure. I told him—because I wanted him not to get it—that he was counting his chickens, but as I say he was obsessed. He took Rex Belton to look over the place and made all sorts of plans."

"We saw his rough sketches."

"He did those that first night."

"They were very good."

"He was sort of artistic. He was a good photographer, too. That's what frightened me. You see, Johnny had knocked about for years, doing deals, and he'd really got nothing to show for it. I knew he wanted to make a killing and his obsession showed me that he thought this was his big chance."

Masters nodded to show he understood. "Now," he said quietly, "we come to Mr Melada's disappearance and how it came to dawn on you that he was dead."

She put the dog down and got to her feet. "Would you like coffee?" she asked.

"I'm sure Sergeant Berger could get it for us. He's a very good coffee maker and being a good detective I feel sure he'll be able to locate the necessary items in your kitchen."

Green looked across at Masters as though he mistrusted the tone the Superintendent had used. The girl had been talking for long enough. It was natural she should need a break which making coffee would afford her. But Masters wasn't for letting her off the hook. As far as Green knew, Berger had never made coffee. So what was going on? Berger, however, took the hint as an order and made his way into the adjoining kitchen. As there was no door it wasn't difficult to find."

"When did Mr Melada not come home?" asked Masters.

"Two nights after he spoke to the Brigadier and was

told his bid for the church had been bettered by somebody else."

"Were you surprised?"

"Not particularly."

"Why not? Was he in the habit of staying away overnight without letting you know?"

"It happened. But always before—if he hadn't let me know—he'd arrived home in the middle of the next morning."

"Did he say where'd he been on these occasions?"

"He didn't have to. He was always shamedfaced and laughing, apologetic perhaps but insincere, and he never bothered to supply anything but the lamest of excuses."

"You suspected other women?"

"With Johnny? Always. He drank very little and he never gambled on horses or cards, so what could he have been up to?"

"Perhaps the cash deals you mentioned earlier."

She shook her head. "Not when he didn't tell me. He was a sucker for any hard-luck story, and he'd help any of his mates who asked him. And that involved him in all manner of activities ranging from painting a bedroom to an excursion to the continent to rescue and bring back the motor car of an acquaintance who had fallen foul of the Dutch police and was to be kept in jail in Holland for heaven knows how long."

"On such occasions you were always told what was afoot?"

"Usually by telephone, after he'd got roped in."

"But no message reached you this time?"

"No. And I didn't suspect a woman that time."

"Why not?"

"He wasn't in the mood for one."

"I'll take your word for it. When did you really start to worry?"

"By mid-afternoon. By then, in the past, he had always either returned or he had phoned. This time he had done neither."

139

"So you began to worry?"

"Yes."

"What about, specifically? His whereabouts? Or his health?"

"Both."

"Why his health?"

"His attitude, ever since he had learned that his offer for the church had been outbid, made me think there was something seriously wrong."

"More seriously wrong than you would have expected at just being outbid?"

"Yes. After his offer had been turned down, he was angry. Very angry. That surprised me because he was never angry. He laughed everything off, usually."

"But you must have been glad his offer was turned down."

"I was. I tried not to let it show, though, because I didn't want to make him more angry."

"Did you succeed?"

"Yes. He went very quiet after that. And thoughtful. As though he were thinking through some complicated plan."

"Did he tell you what it was?"

"No."

"Did you ask?"

"No. I daren't. You see, he had stopped laughing and that made me realise that I'd be silly to poke my nose in."

"Did he do anything?"

"Not until the next afternoon. He went out in the car and was away for about two and a half hours. He came back for supper and then went out again without any explanation. I didn't ask any questions because, though I felt satisfied that the business of buying the church was over with no real harm done, I didn't want to upset him. But because I didn't ask him and he didn't tell me, I was totally unaware of what his movements were or what he was thinking about so deeply." She pushed her glasses up her nose. "Can't you understand? I didn't like his mood. He was so quiet he was either threatening or—if I was wrong about that—morose. I couldn't decide because I'd never seen him like it before. But whichever it was it made me worry like hell when he didn't come home that night."

Berger came in with a wooden tray on which were five mugs of black coffee, a milk bottle and a sugar bowl. With great courtesy he offered it to Happy first, asked if she would like milk and on being told that she would, poured it in for her. Green got up. "You may fancy yourself as a French waiter, lad, but it'll be quicker if we help ourselves. I'm clammed. I could drink a gallon of this."

Masters waited until everybody was settled again and Goliath had chosen a patch of carpet full in the sun, and then asked: "What did you do after the middle of the afternoon of the day on which he did not come home? You said that was when you really started to worry."

"At about four o'clock I rang Rex Belton. Or tried to."

"Please explain."

"Rex was a commercial traveller for an agricultural implements firm. Johnny always told me that Rex cheated. He never worked in the afternoons. He was always at home watching telly. But if the phone rang, his wife, Carol, always answered it so she could say he was out, unless it was Johnny, and then she'd put Rex on."

"Mrs Belton answered your ring and told you her husband was not at home?"

"That's right."

"She knew who it was calling?"

"I told her. She didn't even say when he'd be back or ask if she could take a message. It seemed funny to me that on the one day I wanted him, Rex was not at home, because Johnny rang him most days."

"Did you and Mrs Belton know each other well?"

"Very well. Johnny and Rex were the great friends, but the four of us were out together at least once a week and we visited each other's houses."

"So Mrs Belton's attitude over the phone seemed strange."

"So strange I said I thought Rex was always at home in the afternoons and she said usually, in a tone which would have frozen me if I hadn't been at the other end of a phone line. But I went on. I said I wasn't after her husband. I only wanted to know if he had seen Johnny. And she asked me if I meant today. I said or last night as I hadn't seen Johnny since half past seven and she said Rex was at home last night.

"It seemed funny to me. Rex doesn't stop at home. If nothing else he goes out to the pub, so I asked her if she meant he hadn't gone out and she said she meant he had come home in time to go to bed and he hadn't mentioned Johnny. So I asked her if something was wrong as she seemed so strange and upset, but she said there was nothing the matter. When I asked when she was expecting Rex she said she had really no idea."

"What then? Did you ring off?"

"Of course not. I asked her—when he came in—to ask him to ring me. She didn't like that because she thinks Rex goes for me, which he does, but only because I'm not married to him. Only she can't see that. So she asked me why I wanted him to ring. I told the silly cow I wanted to ask him or tell him about Johnny. After all, they were great mates. She said she would tell Rex, but she didn't expect he'd know where John was. And then she said that by now I ought to know what John was and her advice to me was to leave him.

"Then she went on about how she and Rex had known Johnny far longer than I had and he's always been the same with women. Of course, I was angry by then so I asked her how she knew. Did he have a tumble with her— or worse—wouldn't he have one with her? She went all hoity-toity and said she would forget I'd said that now that Johnny had left me and then she rang off."

"Did you wonder what she'd meant by that remark about Mr Melada leaving you?"

"Did I not! I was left with a very strong feeling that Carol had been aware of Johnny's disappearance before

I phoned her. She could only have got such information from Rex, so it meant the two of them had been talking since the night before even though Rex had only got home in time to go to bed and he'd been out all that day. I know I was worried at the time and probably a bit too sensitive but I couldn't help wondering whether they'd been speculating that Johnny had gone...gossiping...or speaking from sure knowledge."

"So what did you do?"

"I looked to see if Johnny had taken anything with him. The car had gone. I knew that. But nothing else. So he hadn't intended to stay away. At eight o'clock I rang the Beltons again. Carol answered and said Rex wasn't home yet but I didn't believe her because there was none of the worry in her voice that there would have been if Rex had been hours overdue on his selling area which is within a thirty-mile radius. I mean she would have been worried, wouldn't she, if she hadn't known where he was, in view of the fact that his best friend was missing?"

"Good point, that," said Green approvingly.

"There could have been a link-up—a connection that any woman whose husband was overdue would never miss."

"So," said Masters, "you were convinced that Mr and Mrs Belton knew more than they were prepared to reveal."

"I guess I was. I went to bed at midnight, but I didn't go to sleep. I had lots of facts to juggle with. Johnny had never gone away for so long before without letting me know. Rex Belton had never been unavailable before. And in view of the fact that I had asked him to call me, I'd have expected him to ring."

"What if his wife hadn't told him?"

"Even if Carol didn't tell him I wanted to speak to him, she would have talked about Johnny's latest escapade. And Rex would have rung to see if there was any news. Rex would have rung anyway, because the two of them were so close I never remember a day on which they

143

didn't get in touch with each other. And as none of this had happened, I was certain Rex and Carol had something to hide. Something serious."

"So what did you do? Go to their house?"

"I remembered it was Friday coming up and Friday is Carol's shopping day in Lincoln. As regular as clockwork. Rex knew all the farmers round about, so he kept a deep freeze stocked with meat and vegetables, so she only went in for other things. She could always get them all into a wheeled shopper which she took with her on the bus.

"So I made a decision. I knew where Carol would be at precisely what time. I decided to waylay her and demand to know what she and Rex were keeping from me. Face to face with me, I thought, she'd be a lot more vulnerable than on the end of a phone line.

"I had to cycle in. It's less than three miles. I was in good time to park the Chopper and take up a position in a shop doorway from which I could see the bus stop. But she wasn't on the bus and there wouldn't be another for an hour. And what made me think even more. Was there any significance in the fact that Carol had broken an unbreakable habit on that particular day? Anyhow, I walked away, thinking about it. Then I saw Rex's car. The only reason I noticed it was because the driver was having difficulty in manoeuvring it into the last remaining space on the other side of the road. I thought my chance to get hold of Rex had come, but I suddenly saw it wasn't Rex driving. It was Carol. And I knew that was odd, because Friday morning was a busy morning for Rex, and he couldn't do his work without his car.

"I followed Carol. She went into Boots and straight to the medicines counter. She had to wait a bit because the early patients at surgeries were waiting with prescriptions. So I was able to get up close. I heard her ask for tincture of Arnica, Witch Hazel, sticking plasters and some brand of ointment. And that was something for me to chew over. Rex and Carol have no kids and there was nothing wrong with Carol, so the medicines had to be for Rex who, remember, wasn't at work. So I knew that the chemist's run had been made on Rex's behalf, and Carol's purchases were all for the treatment of sprains and contusions and bruises. Which meant that Rex had either been in an accident or a fight. I ruled out accident, because I'd just seen the car and that was all right, so I had no hesitation in assuming it had been a fight. And I guessed I knew who with."

"With your husband?"

"Yeah! With Johnny. Only Johnny hadn't come home and the Beltons were hiding things. Do you wonder I thought Johnny was hurt or—seeing he hadn't got in touch with me—dead?"

There was a silence.

At last—

"Did you approach Mrs Belton?"

"No. I wanted to think, so I let her go."

"And have you spoken to her since?"

"No. I didn't ring them. I reckoned I'd wait to see what Rex would do. I reckoned if he didn't ring, he'd killed Johnny."

"And he didn't ring?"

"No."

"But, Chief," said Berger, "she accused Belton of murdering Melada."

"So she did. But even if I knew she was right, what could I do about it? Belton is dead, too."

The car turned out of the lane in the direction of the Beltons' house. Berger said: "So he is. You know, I'd forgotten that for the moment."

"I'm not surprised, lad," said Green. "I nearly did myself. I was so taken up with that lass's clever thinking I forgot everything else."

"And I'm guilty, too," said Masters. "I forgot to ask her what happened to Melada's car. He had it with him when he went out that last night. Reed, remember to ask Mr Webb what became of it."

"And Belton's and Heberden's, Chief?"

"Yes. We're half asleep, not to have asked where they are before this."

"Homer nods," said Reed. "You can't ask every question and get an answer inside forty-eight hours in a case like this."

"We haven't answered any questions," said Green.

"I thought you just agreed that what we've just been told answers the question of who killed Melada."

"It probably does, but *we* didn't answer it. *She* did. And even she couldn't tell us why two good mates had a fight which ended in one being killed by the other."

The journey was less than a mile and took only a minute or two. The Belton house was a traditional semi-detached, as neat and well-painted as one could have wished.

"I bet he got his rose bushes free," said Green as they went through the iron gate. "Just look at them. Peace, Alamein and Carnival. Some garden centre proprietor came up with those for favours received, I'll bet."

The door had a dolphin knocker besides a bell push which gave a two-tone signal when Masters touched it. The door opened and a woman of what Masters judged to be about thirty-five years of age answered the door. She had carefully coiffeured, brassy hair, blue-tinted rimless spectacles and long, dangling earrings. She wore a navy blue linen dress with a frilly blouse beneath it, and matching high-heeled shoes. She was not a big woman, but well built with a long face and longish nose, carefully coated with too-pink a powder to be natural, while the prim mouth was over reddened with lipstick.

"Mrs Belton? We are policemen."

"You'd better come in. I don't want the neighbours staring."

She turned and went ahead. Berger whispered to Reed: "I should think after being married to that, Belton would prefer young Happy."

The sitting-room held a three piece suite, a piano and a stool. Berger got the stool. Green and Reed shared the settee.

146

"Have you got whoever killed my Rex?" demanded Carol Belton for starters.

"Madam," said Masters firmly, "there are three deaths to investigate. They only came to light within the last forty-eight hours. We are making progress. The discovery of the two other bodies after that of your husband shows that."

"I shall want whoever murdered my Rex properly punished."

"Murdered, Mrs Belton? We're not sure about that."

"Not sure? How else did he die?"

"That's just the point, ma'am, we don't know how he died."

"Don't know. They told me he'd been pushed down a well."

"His dead body was. But that isn't what killed him."

"Rex was a healthy man."

"Mr Melada was a big man. Perhaps he killed Mr Belton."

"John Melada? But he was dead before...."

"Before your husband, ma'am? Now how would you know that?"

"I wouldn't...I mean, I didn't...."

"Of course not. Mr Melada disappeared before your husband, so you automatically assumed he died first. A very natural mistake. And you're probably right. So if not Mr Melada, then who would want to kill Mr Belton?"

"Nobody I know of. Mr Belton was a well-thought-of man."

"I feel sure he was. But as we policemen know to our cost, even respectability has its enemies these days."

Green joined in. "That's true enough, ma'am. Even to look respectable like—well, like you do—causes some people a great deal of envy these days. They don't know how to behave and live like you obviously do, ma'am. Your neat house with its tidy garden and beautifully pressed curtains...they rouse enmity in certain quarters."

Berger was staring at Green open-mouthed. Masters caught his eye and frowned a warning to play up. Mrs

Belton was warming to flattery. "Ah, yes! There are no standards these days. Nobody wants to help themselves."

"Unless it's to the other people's property," added Masters.

"That's what I always said to Rex."

"About John Melada, perhaps?"

"Well, he's dead now, but John was naughty. He never kept a job for long."

"And he lived with a woman who wasn't his wife."

"Yes."

"It must have been very difficult for you to accept them as friends, Mrs Belton, even if only for your husband's sake."

"Yes, I had to tolerate them because they were, as you say, Rex's friends."

"Well, now, Mrs Belton, as you can't tell us who might have wanted to harm your husband, perhaps you will be able to tell us something of what he did during those last days. Now I understand that Mr Melada tried to buy the church where the bodies were found and that he took Mr Belton along to see it."

"He did. Rex came back and told me all about it."

"Fine. Now, Mrs Belton, I'm sure you will appreciate that as the church is where the bodies were found, it plays an important part in our investigation, so I'm going to ask you to tell us as exactly as you can what your husband told you about that visit. It could be very important."

Mrs Belton smoothed her skirt and settled herself. "Where shall I begin?"

"It was in the afternoon, wasn't it?"

"Oh yes, that's right. It was about a week after John had made a bid for the church. He'd asked Rex to go along to see the property and to tell him what the things inside were worth."

"Your husband was a valuer, Mrs Belton?"

"No, but he was a good business man and had so many contacts, you see. Rex knew everybody worth knowing. All the big landowners and farmers, and he was always doing bits of business for them."

"I'm sure he was and it shows he was trusted in the community."

"So he went along with John. I remember he told me John was awfully pleased because some legal notices to do with the sale had been put up.

"Rex said he wasn't very impressed by the church. Well, he wouldn't be, would be? Not a draughty old church after a nice home. It would be different for John—after living in that old shack, I mean.

"Rex looked round and he told John that the pews would fetch a pretty penny and he even offered to arrange the sale if John wanted him to. But John said he'd need the timber for balcony supports and staircases. Of course Rex wasn't bothered one way or the other, seeing he was only out to do John a favour, but he did ask him not to destroy priceless pews for the cost of the wood. Rex said he could get him a load of timber for less than he could sell one of those pews for."

"A very useful offer, ma'am. Did Mr Melada accept?"

"Rex wasn't sure. John said if he let Rex do what he wanted it would make the deal self-financing and that would please Happy, although he said he didn't think Happy would see it like that."

"What then?"

"I think Happy must have spoken to Rex about it, because Rex said to John that Happy mistrusted John's motives. Ulterior they were, said Rex, but John said not ulterior motive but profit motive was the name of the game."

"Was that all?"

"No. Rex came back quite angry. He said he'd told John that Happy thought that he, John, was getting tired of her and once he'd got the place set up he'd use it as a love-nest for himself among other things. And that would be the end for Happy. Rex believed Happy. John always was a womaniser and he'd lived with Happy for four years, so of course he wanted a change. He'd seized on the church as a good way of doing it. Of course John denied it, but Rex didn't believe him. He knew John too well. He knew he'd been with other women while living with Happy and it stood to reason a dowdy little thing like her couldn't hold on to a man like John Melada for ever."

"So they quarrelled?"

"Just a bit. More than they'd ever done before."

"Your husband took Happy's part. Did he like her?"

"He didn't want to see her hurt."

"Very commendable of him. What happened next? Surely that wasn't the end of the friendship between the two men?"

"It was almost. They met in a pub one night and I think things were back to normal."

"Was that before Mr Melada knew he had been outbid for the church?"

"Oh yes. Yes, I think so."

"Surely your husband must have told you: would have told you if Mr Melada had said a bigger bid had been put in?"

"He didn't."

"I see. How soon after that was it that Mrs Melada rang to ask to speak to your husband? The night you said he was out?"

"I'm not sure."

"Please try to think, Mrs Belton. Was it the next night or two nights after?"

"When she rang? In the afternoon?"

"Yes."

"That was two days after Rex had seen John."

"Mr Melada had not returned home the night before. And your husband had only arrived home in time to go to bed. Wasn't that unusual?"

"Well, yes."

"Where had he been?"

"Out...with some customers. Oh, I don't know."

"You didn't ask him?"

"No."

"Not even though he came home hurt and you had to dress his wounds that night, all the next day and then the next morning, Friday, you had to go into Lincoln not for your usual groceries, but to replenish your medicine chest with Arnica, Witch Hazel, plasters and ointment?"

The dismay in her face might have been comical at any other time. Now it was pitiful. These men had known. Had known all the time. Her mouth had dropped open.

"How...?" she began. "How did you know that?"

"How we know is our affair, Mrs Belton. You used your husband's car, so he wasn't at work. He'd been at home ever since the night Melada disappeared, hadn't he?"

There was no need for her to say yes.

"Did he fight with Melada?"

She nodded.

"What about?"

No reply.

"Come now, Mrs Belton. Your husband was doing one of his bits of business for his customers, wasn't he? He was acting as agent for Alexander Heberden who had outbid Melada for the church. Melada had got to know or guessed. Is that right?"

"He'd guessed," she whispered. "He said nobody knew about his bid except the office in Lincoln, the vicar and Happy, besides Rex and me. So it had to be one of us. He said he recognised Rex's style or handiwork or something. Rex was the only one who knew Heberden and himself...."

"He knew it was Heberden?"

"Oh yes. He'd asked who'd collected the key from the pub where it was kept."

"Of course. But how did he get your husband to go to the churchyard?"

"I asked Rex that, and he said John didn't. He followed him there."

"Your husband was going?"

"Yes."

"Why, Mrs Belton?"

151

"I don't know."

"Come along, Mrs Belton, why was he going there?"

"To pick something up, I think." It was said in a whisper.

"He didn't collect the key that night?"

"No."

"So what he went to collect was in the churchyard?"

"I suppose so."

"Something he had put there? Taken from the church and hidden for collection at a time when Heberden wasn't with him? Something he wasn't entitled to but which he reckoned had a market value and which Heberden would never miss?"

"It was only a little praying desk. A pre-something or another, Rex called it. A little carved oak thing."

"A prie-dieu?"

"That was it."

"Where is it now?"

By this time she was in tears. "Rex burnt it. Broke it up and burned it in the garden incinerator."

Masters' lips tightened. "He brought it home and destroyed it? Why? Because he knew it would link him with Melada's death if he kept it or sold it?"

She nodded miserably. "He didn't kill John. There was a fight. John started it. He went up to Rex and accused him of doing him dirt. Rex told him he had only done it because Happy had asked him to try and stop John buying the church."

"I'll accept that. But as persuasion wouldn't work, your husband saw another way to stop Melada, and at the same time to make a bit of money for himself?"

She nodded again. "John was bigger and stronger than Rex. Rex got hit about the face and he said John would have beaten him up badly. But then John stumbled over something in the long grass and hit his head on a gravestone. Rex thought he was just knocked out, but he wasn't. He was dead."

"I see. So your husband panicked, instead of going to

the police. He buried the body."

"He always had samples of tools in the car. He had a spade."

"I see. He buried Melada, picked up the pre-dieu which he knew was not only covered in his prints but which he knew the police would discover could only have been moved by him, and came home to you?"

"He was in an awful state. I looked after him, but he couldn't go to work for the next two days, and after that it was the weekend to give him more time. But that girl kept ringing up to talk to him and tell him John was missing...."

"I know," said Masters sympathetically. "It must have been a terrible and worrying time for you."

"And then...and then...."

"Yes?"

"I'd got him all healed up and nothing had happened about John, so we were feeling a bit safer. He went out on the Wednesday evening and...and he just never came back."

"And you've no idea where he was going or why?"

"I don't know anything about it, except that he was quite worried. He said he'd got another job on. I told him to forget it, but he said it wouldn't wait."

Masters got to his feet.

"My advice to you, Mrs Belton, is to try to forget all about it. I know that will be difficult, and it may be that we shall have to take a complete statement from you. But we shall do our best to keep things quiet. After all, we can't proceed against your husband, so there will be little point in pursuing the matter. We shall do our best. You do yours. If and when the statement is taken, hold nothing back. Make a clean breast of it. You will feel better and a lot of the worry will go."

"Rex wasn't a murderer."

"That's just as well," said Green, "otherwise you might have been taken up as an accessory."

* * *

"Where to now, Chief?"

"What's the time? Twenty to one? Back to our hotel. We'll see Mrs Heberden this afternoon."

"I wonder if there's beef pie on the menu?" murmured Green.

— 7 —

She was between fifty and fifty-five by Masters' guess. Her face showed it, but her figure didn't. She was gracious, in attitude, in movement, in manners. Her husband had been found, less than twenty-four hours earlier, dead in a sealed tomb built for one of his ancestors—killed in a way nobody as yet knew how—and yet she met her visitors as though they were welcome guests in normal life. Her hair was greying, but attractively coiffeured. Her summer frock was of simple cut, in well-pressed flowered cotton. She ushered them into the sitting-room and seated them in chintz-covered chairs that had seen years of service and offered still more.

"We're on a melancholy errand, ma'am," said Masters.

"You're on an errand at a melancholy time," she said so gently as not to make it appear a correction. "That is certainly not your fault, and I understand I am in your debt."

"How, ma'am?"

"For finding Alexander. You do realise, don't you, that had he not been found now, it is possible that he would always have been thought of as missing and I would have been left in a state of uncertainty and doubt for ever." She smiled a little. "You see, I can't think that anybody else would have bought St John's and, even had they done so, that they would have uncovered the tomb after finding it sealed so firmly."

"If the discovery has relieved your mind in any way, ma'am, we are very pleased."

She got to her feet, picked up an onyx cigarette box

155

from a coffee table and handed it round. Masters declined, saying he preferred a pipe. She asked him to smoke it if he wished.

It was all far more easy-going than Masters had dared hope. Green was at his most affable, heavily gallant. He didn't address Mrs Heberden as love or lass, but he got close to it, as though to indicate that she and he were of the same generation.

"We've been wondering," he said, "why Mr Heberden bought that church. We know, of course, that it's been connected with the family since the year spit, but it's been standing empty, available and for sale for years."

"As you say, Mr Green, it has been our church for—as my grandson would say—yoinks. But Alexander, who wasn't a great churchman, though he was, I believe, a good Christian, was quite content that it should remain empty."

"He told you so?"

"He never mentioned it. Had he had ideas on the subject or had even thought about it, he would have talked to me. As we never discussed it, I feel safe in saying he was content that it should remain as it was, unused."

"So what made him change his mind?"

"The man Belton, who sometimes called on him to discuss farm machinery, told him a story which disturbed him greatly."

"And what was that, ma'am?"

"That the church was to be sold off very cheaply under the pretext that it was to be turned into a holiday retreat for artists. But, in fact, this pretext was to be a cover for the setting up of something much less desirable. Probably for the making of pornographic films and the production of scatological literature.

"As I said, he was a good Christian. By that I meant that he believed in standards and principles and lived up to them. Inbred in him was a sense—a protective sense—as far as our part of the country was concerned. He believed it was his duty to prevent the influx of people and, if you like, industries, which would have a deleterious effect on our area or indeed on the country as a whole."

"So why didn't he object to the Redundant Churches Commission?"

"Because to have done so without proof of his allegations would have been libellous. Before one could object one would have to have proof that the undesirable act was proceeding. Or at any rate, that is how Alexander viewed the matter. He didn't want to be sued for defamation."

"He thought it would be cheaper to buy the church?"

"Most assuredly he did when Mr Belton said he could get it for him for as little as five thousand pounds."

"Plus a little something as an agent's fee."

"Naturally."

"Would it surprise you to know that the man whom your husband outbid had only offered two thousand and would most certainly have got what he wanted had your husband not intervened?"

"I wonder why Belton told Alexander to bid five thousand when, say, two thousand five hundred would have done the trick? There would be nothing more in it for Belton as agent."

"That's easy," said Green. "Melada was proposing to raise three thousand for modernising the place. Perhaps he had raised some of it and had told Belton how much. Belton wanted to make sure your husband's bid topped everything Melada could rake up."

"I think I understand." She was hesitant.

"Don't try, lady. The games these wheelers and dealers get up to are beyond the comprehension of such as you. But more to the point, can you tell us why your husband should have gone to the church that evening?"

"I'm afraid not. I was away at the time."

"Have a guess. Was there anything urgent he wanted to do there that he'd told you about?"

"Just the opposite. He said he wasn't even going to think about it until after all the summer shows were over. Then it would give him something to do in the winter."

"Turning it into a music centre?"

She smiled. "That was largely my idea. I approved of buying the church, but I definitely thought that once we owned it we should do something with it."

"Has the sale been finally settled?"

"Not yet. But I shall go through with it. I shall turn it into some sort of cultural centre in memory of Alexander."

"A wise idea, ma'am."

She looked at Masters. "It's a little early, perhaps, but it is hot. Could I offer you tea?"

"You certainly could. We shall be delighted to join you."

They were back in Webb's office by five o'clock. Masters waited until a few minutes past the hour before ringing Watling, to give the pathologist a little leeway in case he had overslept.

Watling wasted no words. "I have my colleague here with me, Superintendent, and also his written report. His answers are exactly the same as mine. He, too, has been unable to isolate in either of the two bodies presented to us a cause for the fatal respiratory depression. That's it officially. Unofficially, we're bloody well stumped."

"Thank you, doctor. It was what I expected so I'm not disappointed."

"I am. I wish we could have helped."

"In that way, so am I. But you know what I meant. Thank you for all the work you and your colleague have done. It has been very useful."

"You're joking, of course."

"Not at all. At least you established what it wasn't. We haven't had to hare round the countryside looking for supplies of strychnine or arsenic or whatever."

"There's that, I suppose. But it's a bit negative, isn't it?"

"True. But even negatives are facts, and facts are what we both rely on."

"I'm pleased you can take it so well. How are things going? Still keeping up the good work?"

158

"I believe we are. The pace may not have been quite so hot as yesterday, in that we haven't uncovered any more dead bodies, but we've moved along a bit. When I see you I'll explain."

"You propose to call on me?"

"I have it in mind."

"When? And what for?"

"I expect the day after tomorrow, though I can't guarantee that."

"What for?"

"I can't tell you yet. It's just an idea I have. I think I'd like to clarify things in my mind and then try it out on you."

"As you wish. You'll always be welcome and I'll give you any help I can."

"You're very generous. Goodbye, doctor."

"What was all that about?" asked Green who had been standing by during the phone call.

"It will take a session to tell you, Greeny. I want the help of your prodigious memory as well as your help in doing a number of jobs here."

"Here? You say that as though you'll be somewhere else."

"Depending on what comes out of our session, I may be. Reed and I may have to go to London for the day tomorrow. We'll take the train and leave the car with you and Berger."

"It's not just a swan, is it?" queried Green.

"You'll be able to judge that for yourself after we've talked. Right now, I think we'd better put Webb and Iliff in the picture. I don't want them to feel left out just because they weren't with us today. And by the time we've finished with them it'll be time for a bath and a change and a long, cold drink before dinner."

"Now you're talking. Let's get weaving. And incidentally...."

"Yes?"

"What's wrong with a long, cold drink before a bath as well as after?"

"You'll be wanting one during your bath next."

"Not a bad idea, that."

They talked in Masters' room after dinner. Green sprawled in the armchair, Masters on the bed.

"I want the benefit of your elephantine memory, Greeny."

"Oh yes? What about?"

"Sometime—within the last twelve months, I think—there was a fatal accident to a veterinary surgeon reported."

"That's right. He'd accidentally injected himself with some drug he was shoving into an animal. From what I remember of the account, such accidents are by no means unknown, but when they're using the really strong drugs they're supposed to have another syringe ready filled with antidote. So they can bung it into themselves, or their assistants can, if the animal rears at the wrong moment and the vet himself gets the shot intended for the horse or cow or whatever."

"That's what I wanted to know. Any more?"

"I think the reporters dragged in accounts of previous accidents where the vet had been saved after the precautious had been taken."

"Fine." Masters took from his inside pocket the list of drugs that had been lost when Marchant's surgery had been blown up. "Cast your eyes down that lot. I want to know if any of the names ring a bell."

"As the drug that was being used in the case we've been talking about?"

"Yes. I'm sure the drug in question was mentioned."

"It was," admitted Green, "but I don't remember its name." He looked down the list very carefully, taking his time, seeing if any of the names caused any slight stirrings of memory. Masters sat quietly, watching his colleague's face, hoping to see recognition dawn on his features. At

160

length, Green looked up. "Nothing here," he said. "Not a bloody sausage. All those chemical names are beyond me. I don't even know how to pronounce most of them, let alone remember them after a year."

"Not to worry. It was just a chance."

"Of what?"

"That one of those drugs was nicked and used on Belton and Heberden."

"Oh no, you don't! Watling and his pal both swear there was no injection sites on those bodies and no signs of drugs having been taken by mouth."

"Agreed. But listen for a few minutes will you?"

"Go ahead."

Masters spoke for nearly twenty minutes. From time to time Green interposed a question or grunted his agreement. When Masters finished he said: "It's so bloody far-fetched it could just be true."

"You admit it would link all the strange happenings round here recently."

"If you're right, it will."

"So we've got to try."

Green nodded. "But you'll still be short of proof."

"That's where you and Berger come in." Masters spoke for a few more minutes, outlining what he wanted Green to do, and ended with, "And use forensic if you need to."

Green nodded. "What time are you going?"

"I want Berger to run us into Lincoln for the first train. Reed should have got the times. We'll probably be away about six. No need for you to get up. Stay and have a decent breakfast."

"I intend to. Phone through to Webb's office to tell us when you want picking up."

Masters stood up. "There's still an hour of legitimate drinking time left."

"What are we waiting for?"

When he and Reed reached the Yard the next morning, Masters said to the sergeant: "Ask the librarian for the

161

RSM tickets. I'll be in my office."

"Sorry, Chief! RSM?"

"Royal Society of Medicine library. You'll have to sign for it."

"Sign for a library ticket?"

"When I was a sergeant," said Masters, "the Yard could just afford one of those tickets."

"Afford?"

"They were a hundred quid a year then. Heaven knows what they cost now."

"Right, Chief. I'll call for an armed squad to come with me."

Masters spent some time in his office with the list of drugs and his private copy of Martindale. When Reed joined him he asked the sergeant to order coffee and then returned to his work. It took a long time, but eventually, long after the coffee had arrived and been consumed, he gave a small cry of satisfaction.

"Bingo, Chief?"

"I think so." He whistled through his teeth. "No wonder there were no hypodermic marks. They weren't needed."

"You've lost me, Chief."

"Have I? Never fear, Reed, all will be revealed. Time to go." He made a note in his pocket book and got to his feet. "Library ticket?"

"Safe and sound, Chief," said Reed, patting his jacket.

"Good. We'll take a cab."

Inside the RSM, Masters explained what he wanted and was willingly given the help necessary to find the references he mentioned, together with a number of others allied to the subject. He spent over an hour at one of the reading tables going through the journals carefully. Some he handed over to Reed who dutifully ploughed through the papers indicated, but not understanding them fully because much of the language used was jargon to him and he hadn't the temerity to interrupt Masters to ask for explanations. Masters had not such qualms, and from time to time approached the librarian for the meanings of

TLC, EMIT and various other combinations of letters unrecognisable to the layman.

But by and large, Reed got the drift. He was amazed by what he read and by the fact that Masters had managed to hit on this at all. It made Reed imagine that he would never be able to emulate Masters. But the Superintendent, when Reed put his thought to him during one of the brief breaks in Masters' reading, told him not to be a fool because it was totally on account of his, Reed's, work at the vet's that he, Masters, had got on to this particular line of enquiry. This made Reed feel better even though he privately reckoned that to make the mental jump from a list of missing products to a research session at a library like this was not likely to be achieved by most of the men he knew at the Yard.

By one o'clock Masters had chosen three pieces of material and asked if he could have them photocopied. The librarian he approached was helpful and they were able to go off to lunch with the work satisfactorily completed. Throughout the meal and the train journey back to Lincoln in the afternoon, Masters was uncommunicative. Recognising the signs, Reed made no attempt to interrupt Masters' thoughts until they were approaching their destination.

"Nearly there, Chief."

Masters, a dead pipe in his mouth, nodded, and stood up to take his briefcase from the rack.

"Is it all sewn up, Chief?"

"I'm hoping so. Oh, yes, we know all about it now, but getting the proof is going to be the tricky bit, don't you think?"

"Proof of what, Chief?"

Masters looked at him. "You haven't fathomed it yet?"

"How it was done? I think so. But not who did it."

Green had not come in the car to meet them. He was sitting in the bar of The Chestnut Tree when they entered the hotel.

"I saw you coming, so I lined them up."

"Thanks."

"Do we drink to victory or to drown our sorrow?"

"My end came out all right. What about yours?"

Green took a gulp of beer before replying.

"Fine. But there's no hard fact."

"The optician?"

"Just as you thought."

"Cars?"

"There's the problem."

"Not found?"

Green shook his head. "The area is being combed by the locals, but we haven't discovered them."

"Where have they looked?"

Green shrugged. "Everywhere they can think of. The favourite would be water, but look at the map and you'll see there are no lakes or gravel pits of any size. Plenty of small water courses, but none of them big enough to take three cars."

"Garages and lock-ups?"

"They're making enquiries in all the villages and in Lincoln itself. But it's a hell of a job. There are so many old yards and old sheds."

"So what do we do?"

"Can't make bricks without straw," said Green philosophically and finished his beer without waiting for comment on his remark.

Masters looked across at him with an exclamation of annoyance.

"Now what have I said wrong?" asked Green.

"Not you. Me."

"What?"

"There won't be three cars to find. At least there will, but not altogether. Belton must have got rid of Melada's."

Green knocked his forehead with the heel of his hand. "Of course. And I didn't see that, either." He turned to Berger. "Or you, laddo."

"Or any of the locals, either," retorted Berger.

"They're not in the know," said Green. "You are."

164

Berger shrugged. "If you ask me, he must have used his missus to help. After Melada died, there would be two cars outside the church. He'd drive his own home and rope his wife in...."

"Go on," urged Masters.

"Well, Chief, he'd go back with her. He'd take over Melada's bus while his missus followed to pick up after he'd disposed of it. We know she can drive. She went into Lincoln for those medicines."

"Right," said Green. "Catch the barman's eye, young Berger. I've just got time for one more while you get the car ready."

"Where for?"

"You and me, laddie, we're calling on Mrs Belton."

Carol Belton let them into the house reluctantly. "I've told you all I know," she said plaintively. "Why can't you leave me alone? You promised...."

"Give over," said Green, following her into the too-neat front room. "Sit down and tell us what your old man did with the car."

"What car?"

"Melada's old bus. After Melada died."

She looked at him obstinately.

"Not talking, eh love? Right, we'll go through it step by step. He came home here to get you...."

"No, he didn't."

"No?"

Berger said: "What did he do? Ring up and tell you to catch a bus to somewhere, so's he could pick you up?"

She nodded. "I went to Basset's corner. He was waiting for me."

"Go on."

"He drove back to the church. He picked up Mr Melada's car and...."

"Where did he dump it?"

"In the Walmby brick pit."

"And it hasn't been found?"

"There's water in it."

Green got to his feet. "How much water?"

"I don't know. People round there say it's bottomless."

"It very likely is bottomless," said Masters. "Or nearly so. They dug those pits as much as a hundred feet deep and then when they were played out, left them to fill with water. I remember one when I was a boy. The tall chimney and the ovens were still there. Then one day they blew up the chimney. I watched, from a distance. But I seem to remember that when I was very small, that pit was still in use. It had a hooter, you see, to call the men to work, and I can distinctly remember it sounding every day. But I also remember that I was still quite small when they blew the chimney up, and by that time the pit was full of water. So it must have filled up in about the space of two years." He glanced across at Green. "You said no bricks without straw."

"Aye, I know. Sort of funny that."

"You don't think....?"

"That the other two are down there? Who knows? We'd have to send divers down, and a hundred feet...."

Masters nodded. "Let's have dinner."

"And wait for inspiration?"

Reed said: "The Chief will think of something."

"Not this time," said Masters. "It's a case, I'm afraid for routine slog. It's virtually impossible to think of something or somewhere in unfamiliar country such as this. As witness the DCI. He looked at the map for ponds and lakes and what did he discover? That a car has been dumped in a hundred feet of water which isn't coloured blue on the map because it's a brick pit."

"Quite right," said Green. "It's a case for those who know the area. The village bobbies who pound the beat...."

"Hold it!" said Masters.

Green who was about to sit at the table turned to him. "Now what?"

"It's a case for who?"

"The village bobbies."

"Who pound the beat?"

"Yes. Except they use bicycles round here."

"Pound," said Masters. "Sit down gentlemen and answer me this. If you want to hide something, where do you put it?"

"That's easy," said Green. "I think I'll have the lobster soup followed by the baked fish with leeks au gratin."

"Where?" demanded Masters.

"In the most obvious place."

"Quite. And if you want to hide something from the police?"

"Put in under their noses."

"Where's that?" asked Berger.

"Feel for the bedpost, lad," said Green. "We've been talking about pounding beats, for heaven's sake. Pounding...pound, pound, pound."

Berger's mouth fell open as the penny dropped. "You mean....?"

"That's right, lad. Park a car where you know it will be picked up by the police and towed into a pound where it can stay until it rots for all we care. We don't send out notices: Dear Sir, We have your car, safe and sound, all neatly parked in our pound. There's only fifteen pounds to pay, and you can have it back today."

Masters grinned. "You think there's a possibility I'm right?"

"You damn well know you are. I suppose you want me to ring Webb?"

"No, I'll do it. Go ahead and order. I'll have the same as you. I want Webb to make sure he gets a Scene of Crime officer on to those cars before anybody else starts poking around in them."

"That's if they're there," said Berger.

"They'll be there," said Green, turning and signalling to the waiter. "Here, lad, let's have a bit of service here."

The Yard car pulled up at the Lincoln police station soon after nine o'clock that night. The four were escorted through the station and out to a small yard at the back where they found Webb with two cars and a civilian SCO.

"Anything?" asked Masters.

Webb grinned. "Over and above the red faces among the city mob, do you mean, Chief? You should have seen them. They've been given descriptions and numbers and they've been making enquiries all day. Then you suggest they should look in their pound! Lovely!"

"Has our friend turned anything up?"

Webb called the SCO over.

"I'm taking samples, Superintendent. But what I can tell you straight away is that there's been one of those small-wheeled bikes in both these cars. The marks are there. Heberden's, of course, is a station wagon, so I suppose the cycle went in easier than it did into Belton's Ford. But the wheel marks are there in both. Same pattern tyres as far as I can tell by using a magnifying glass."

"Thank you. When will the samples be tested?"

"Against what?"

"Each other to begin with and against other items of clothing we shall give you tomorrow and, finally, against a house."

"By late tomorrow or the next day if everything's straightforward."

"Thank you. What you've told me so far has been a great help. We'll probably meet again."

The SCO started to assemble his small vacuum cleaner to start taking dust samples from the cars. Webb asked: "How's it going, Chief? Are we getting anywhere at all?"

"Oh, yes. It's all over."

Webb was astounded. "You mean you know who the murderer is?"

"That's right, laddo," said Green. "All signed, sealed and delivered."

"You've made an arrest?"

"We shall leave that for you to do tomorrow," replied Masters. "As the DCI says, we now know how the men were killed and who killed them. But tomorrow morning I want a consultation with Dr Watling before we make a

168

final move. I feel I must have a forensic blessing on this one, because we shall, to some degree, have to rely on circumstantial evidence unless the SCO pulls a lot out of the bag for us."

"You feel you can go ahead before the SCO reports?"

"Yes. Perhaps you would arrange a time for us all to see Watling tomorrow morning. Yourself included. Then you will hear our case and know how to proceed."

Webb shook his head in bewilderment. "I haven't a clue. Not a clue. As to how it was done or who did it. I mean, you've not...."

"Not what, Chum?" asked Green.

"I was going to say, done anything."

"Except talk?"

Webb nodded.

"We found you three bodies, remember."

"And besides," said Masters, "there's still a bit to do."

They crowded into Watling's office the next morning at eleven o'clock. Watling said: "I know you told me you would call on me today, but I didn't expect a deputation as big as this."

"My fault, Doctor, but I felt as I would have to give you the full story, and it's a fairly long gone, it would save time if everybody came to hear what I have to say and your comments on it."

"The full story? We haven't discovered anything."

"We think we have," said Green. "Do you mind if we smoke?"

"You mean," said Watling, pushing over an ash tray, "that you have thought something up which you want to try out on me, or want me to try out for you." He sat back. "It won't work, you know. We've tried everything we can. No results."

"That fact in itself is encouraging," said Masters. "It is a positive indication that the substance we are looking for, and which induced the fatal respiratory depression, is a drug which leaves no trace."

169

"There isn't one," said Watling emphatically.

"I'll put it another way," said Masters. "One that is so powerful and quick acting that, though it would leave traces in anything like a normal dose, can be administered in such small amounts that it will kill before the live body has time to assimilate it or metabolise it, or the bodily organs receive it."

Watling stared hard.

"No," he said quietly. "I don't believe it."

"Hear me out," said Masters, "and then pronounce."

Watling nodded.

"I'm not going to cut corners for you, doctor. I want the others present to hear the full story."

Watling spread his hands. "I'm all ears."

Masters began from the beginning.

"After we discovered Belton's body in the well, and we were waiting for arrangements to be made between the local police and the Yard for us to take over the investigation, Mr Webb told us that not only had he reports of three men missing, but that he'd also had five mysterious fires which seemed to show there was an arsonist at large."

"I'd read about that in the local rag," said Watling.

"That was a coincidence that my team found hard to accept. Mr Webb being so closely involved just accepted that his normal peaceful area had suffered a rash—not necessarily of crime, because at the time there was nothing to cause him to think that the three grown men who had disappeared had all died violent deaths—but of unaccustomed events that needed his attention. As I said, he was closely involved. We were the newcomers who saw most of the game. At least we saw there might be a connection between the various events and, as a result of our discussing the possibility, we decided it would be unwise to ignore the fires."

"I suppose," said Watling, "that if you investigated them and found no connection, nothing would be lost; whereas if you ignored them and it later turned out they were important, you would have been left with egg on your faces."

"That's it. DCI Green undertook that particular job. He made some interesting discoveries. The five fires made a sandwich. The bread and butter on each side was nothing more than four useless old barns and tumbledown hay-stacks. Damage and loss werre minimal. But the meat in the sandwich was a vet's surgery, and there the damage was total and considerable. Mr. Green soon realised that the four minor fires were simply camouflage for the fifth."

"How could he possibly decide that?"

"He very cleverly discovered that the four fires were started by means of using spectacle lenses as burning glasses. But, and this is important, all the fires were started at the same time of day—in the early evening to be precise. Burning glasses can be used at any time of the day as long as the sun is shining, so why early evening? The DCI discovered that only on one day in a week could it be guaranteed that the vet's premises would be vacant, and that was in the evening. So the fire had to be started in the early evening, before the sun went down. In theory, that is. Mr Green came to the conclusion that a burning glass was not used at the surgery. The place was broken into and a fire started under the gas bottles to cause a tremendous explosion. Why? The answer that came to the DCI was that something was to be removed from the surgery and the explosion was to camouflage the theft. We were meant to believe the explosion was the unintentional outcome of the fire.

"So, my sergeants made exhaustive enquiries as to what the surgery had contained, down to the last pill and medical substance the vet could remember. Including the contents and his dangerous substances cupboard.

"The first body found was that of Belton. Though he had been down a well for several days he had not drowned. You, doctor, diagnosed that he had died from respiratory depression, but were unable to find the cause of the condition. The second body found was that of Melada, and there you were able to tell us that he had died as a result of a blow on the head.

"We have confirmed this. Mrs Belton has told us that her husband and Melada fought in the churchyard and that Melada, who was getting the better of the battle, stumbled and struck his head on a tombstone."

"And Belton buried him?"

"In a fit of panic. As an agricultural implements salesman he was accustomed to carrying samples of small tools in his car. He hurriedly buried Melada and then, with the help of his wife, disposed of Melada's car in a flooded brick pit."

"That'd be at Walmby," suggested Webb.

"Quite right. But now we come to the reason for the fight between Melada and Belton. The church of St John the Divine was redundant and up for sale. Melada decided to buy it. His wife didn't wish him to do so on several counts. First she believed they couldn't afford it; second, she disliked the building and the churchyard; and third she feared the uses she thought Melada intended to make of the premises. Belton was her husband's great friend and, secretly, although she herself knew it, an admirer of Happy. Happy asked Belton to help her persuade Melada not to buy the church.

"Normal pressure wouldn't do the trick, but when Belton learned that St John's had strong family connections with the Heberdens, Belton thought he saw a way of pleasing Happy. He knew Heberden—as a business customer—and so approached him with a story. Melada was getting the church very cheaply and intended to turn it into a vice-den. Heberden, a public-spirited man, was keen to stop this. Belton suggested that the easiest way was for Heberden to outbid Melada for the church. As the amount needed would be only five thousand pounds, Heberden agreed and Belton offered to work as his agent.

"Melada was told he had been outbid, and by a bit of clever thinking, came to the conclusion that it was his pal, Belton, who had been instrumental in doing him down. So Melada followed Belton to the church—where he had gone to collect a bit of loot he had stashed away there—

and an argument and the subsequent fight took place.

"So Melada died and was buried. But Happy is a clever little thing. When Melada disappeared, she sought Belton's advice and help. But neither was forthcoming. This roused Happy's suspicions and when she tried to beard Mrs Belton in Lincoln, she discovered that lady buying medicaments for bruises and sprains. As she has no children, Mrs B must have been buying the ointments for her husband. So, reasoned Happy, Mr B had been in a fight and was keeping hidden and wouldn't speak to her on the phone. Which meant that the fight had been with Melada. But Melada would have made mincemeat of Belton in a scrap. Yet Melada was missing. Happy came to the conclusion that somehow Belton had bested Melada, and the non-appearance of the latter could mean only one thing."

"That he was dead?"

Masters nodded. "And she was right, wasn't she?"

"Obviously."

"I told you she was a clever little thing. She has a good degree in zoology and conservation. This would mean she would know something about animals. She decided to put that knowledge to use to gain revenge for Melada's death."

"Happy did?" asked Reed in a shocked voice. "How, Chief, how?"

"You should know. You've done a lot of the spadework and been in on the research. She wears glasses. They become her because she has an endearing little habit of letting them slip down her nose and then pushing them up again. She wears them all the time, so we assumed that she would have to have them changed fairly regularly. It was no great difficulty to find the optician who tests her eyes and supplies her spectacles. The lenses and even parts of lenses discovered at the fires were capable of being measured—something Happy probably did not realise...."

"Or she thought they would be destroyed in the fire," said Green. "Or lost, or not noticed. Maybe she thought nobody would even look for anything at fires in old ricks and barns."

"So she didn't use that method at the vet's surgery?"

"No. She broke in and pinched what she wanted, then lit a fire under the gas bottles. You see, Doc, in a way she was clever. She was going round starting fires, but she didn't even have to carry matches let alone combustible material for four of them. She could have been stopped and searched, even, and the game wouldn't have been given away, because lots of people carry two pairs of spectacles."

Masters continued.

"The focal lengths of the lenses found at the sites of the fires were measured, and in each case they were found to conform to prescriptions which had been made up for Happy in the past. And, incidentally, the lenses in women's spectacles are usually smaller than those men wear. Those found by Mr Green were of the smaller size and of a shape usually associated with women's spectacles.

"So we are fairly sure that Happy was the fire-raiser. She has a Chopper cycle. This would enable her to get around the countryside unobtrusively, and at the moment we are asking questions in the countryside to discover whether a girl on a Chopper was seen anywhere near the sites of any of the fires or, indeed, anywhere around the area. This last because the SCO has already established that such a cycle has been transported in two motor cars found in the city pound. One belonging to Belton and one to Heberden."

"She left them there?" asked Watling.

"No. She left them where she knew they would cause an obstruction and would be impounded by the police."

"I see."

"Now, we have said that to the best of our belief, Happy stole what she wanted from the vet and then set the place on fire to disguise her theft. We have no direct evidence for this claim, but Sergeant Reed, in his list of what the vet kept on the premises, mentioned etorphine."

"Ah!" breathed Watling. "Etorphine hydrochloride."

"Quite. I went through the list, and I found, in my *vade mecum*, that there was very little about etorphine except that it was described as 'unmanageably strong for humans.'"

"I should just think so," said Watling. "It is at least a thousand times stronger than morphine. I mean, when one starts talking about etorphine, one is talking about micrograms of active substance, and you may not all appreciate that a microgram is one millionth of a gram."

"A millionth?" asked Berger. "But that's...that's not measurable. Is it?"

"Decide for yourself. The average aspirin tablet weighs about five hundred milligrams. So you'd have to divide one of those into five hundred to get one milligram. Then you'd have to divide that one grain into a thousand. Of course, it's easier to do in a fluid. You put a tiny drop of active ingredient into a drum of liquid, and then draw off a minute amount of the mixture." He turned to Masters. "I don't know much about etorphine. I've never used it nor encountered it. Officially it is a highly potent analgesic and narcotic for the control of animals—particularly large and fierce ones. What its effects are in man, I wouldn't know from practical experience. But I expect you're going to tell me that, being morphine-like in its action, they will be bradycardia, dizziness, nausea, comas and—dare I say it?—severe respiratory depression?"

"Quite right. Except that in animals you can expect tachycardia and raised blood pressure."

Watling nodded. "I wish I'd listened a little more carefully to you when you suggested that if I were to be given a hint of what I was looking for...."

"It would have made no difference."

"I suppose not."

"Why not?" asked Green.

Masters turned over his papers. "The answer to that is quite long and complicated, but I think I should go into it in full for everybody's sake."

175

"Including mine," said Watling.

"Let me read a little from Martindale. I'll paraphrase, to save time, but it starts: 'The accidental injection of some or all of the contents of a two mil syringe containing etorphine...produced coma in a forty-one year old man. The man was treated with various reversing injections and other supportive measures and he was out of danger in six hours.'" Masters paused and looked around him. "But this is the bit to note: 'It was found later that the syringe contained one mil both before and after the accident. The effects were due to solution present on the needle.'"

Green pursed his lips and hummed. "A weak solution, too, I expect."

"Yes."

"So one sniff of the stuff can knock a bloke out for six hours even when he gets medical attention. So if he doesn't get medical attention, what happens?"

Again Masters turned to his papers. "I've got a couple of published articles from the American National Institute on Drug Abuse. They were using small doses in human guinea pigs—to discover not only its subjective effects but to see what its abuse potential is and to see how well they would detect it in the body. The first paper says it is at least five hundred times as potent as morphine and— please remember this—has a very rapid onset of action. So rapid, in fact, a number of subjects reported effects before the completion of the injection. The paper then goes on to say, in its discussion section, that some researchers had estimated that etorphine is eighty thousand times as potent as morphine. Eighty thousand."

"No wonder it acts rapidly," said Green.

"That was with subcutaneous injection?" asked Watling.

Masters nodded. "So it appears—indeed it is stated in the literature—that spillage on the skin can be dangerous. My information also is that if the skin is broken, a touch by a needle—not a hypodermic needle, but a sewing needle—that has been dipped in etorphine can be fatal if it is laid against broken skin. Now both our bodies had small skin blemishes, I think you said, Doctor, about the arms and hands. Scratches from rose bushes and gardening, wasn't it?"

"Quite right. No hypodermic marks, but plenty of places where an infinitesimal amount of etorphine could have been absorbed."

"But how would she... could she have got it there?" asked Berger.

"Easy," said Green. "Oh, Mr Heberden, what a nasty scratch that is on your arm. Let me look. It seems very angry. Touch with needle. Finish of Heberden. Don't forget neither chap had a jacket on."

"Certainly she wouldn't have to worry about any retaliation, whatever she did," said Masters. "If she actually did as Mr Green said and her victim had objected there would be nothing he could do against a lithe young woman. Don't forget how rapid the onset of action is."

"It gives me the creeps," said Berger.

"Never mind that, lad," said Green. "What I want to know is why the Doc didn't find this stuff in the bodies?"

"I'll deal with that now," replied Masters. "The onset of action is so rapid that vets who propose to use etorphine have to follow a definite safety drill. It goes without saying that they have to use disposable needles and syringes which have to be rinsed thoroughly after use and then stored in a metal box until they can be incinerated. But before loading the etorphine syringe, they must load the syringe of antidote, because there wouldn't be time to do so after an accident. The antidote syringe has to be kept within reach. Now, listen to this. In case there might be a slip or some difficulty in getting the needle into an animal, thereby giving even a remote chance of spillage, vets have first to insert a needle into an animal. Then they fill their syringe with etorphine. Then they disconnect the syringe from the needle in the vial and just screw it on to the one sticking in the animal."

"So they know they won't snap a needle?"

"That's it. I've told you this, so that you will appreciate

177

how powerful etorphine is and how quickly it acts and how quickly help must be given if a man who gets any of it is to be saved. So it follows that if no antidote is used or other help given, a man who takes in etorphine through the skin may be dead—of respiratory depression—in so short a time."

"Wait a minute, Chief," protested Webb. "I'll take everything you've said so far as gospel. But you're asking us to believe these two men died from doses of etorphine, yet forensic—Dr Watling and his colleague, that is—couldn't find any traces of it in the bodies. So how are you going to prove they had it if the pathologists can't swear it was there?"

"Good point, lad," said Green. "Shows you're keeping up with events. Have a fag for being a bright boy."

Webb accepted the cigarette, but eyed Green with a certain amount of mistrust. He suspected his leg was being pulled and in this company he wasn't too sure of himself to begin with. However, his doubts were resolved by Masters who said: "That is a vital and pertinent question, Mr Webb. We shall have to produce a satisfactory answer. I hinted at that when we first arrived, when I said to the Doctor that the fact that he had been unable to trace any drug in the bodies was, in itself, encouraging. These are the points.

"Etorphine acts so rapidly that the bodily functions slow down or even stop before the substance even has time to invade all the organs—liver, kidneys, heart, stomach and so on. Because we mustn't forget that death switches off the mechanisms which transport fluids round the body. That is the first point. The second is that so little etorphine is needed that there is literally not enough to discover in a body—certainly not by normal tests.

"You will recall that I said one of my papers was concerned with the detectabilty of etorphine by the common .screening methods. Perhaps, Dr Watling, you would tell us what urine screening methods you did use."

"Between us, my colleague and I, we used radioimmunoassay, and homogeneous enzyme immunoassy which is known in the trade as EMIT. Then we did analysis by thin-layer chromotography—known as TLC—followed by gas-liquid chromonography, or GLC. I won't go into all the chemistry that accompanies these, but I can say that no sample gave a positive opiate—any kind of opiate, that is—no positive opiate result in either of the two immunoassays, and no etorphine was detected in the TLC and GLC analyses of any urine sample from either of the two men."

"Thank you, doctor. Now I'll give you the gist of the final paragraph of this paper. This is it. 'A dose of one hundred micrograms of etorphine, roughly equivalent to fifty milligrams of morphine, was administered to each of seven subjects.' Now that is some dose, 'and yet etorphine was not detectable in any urine sample by the routine screening procedures of RIA, EMIT, GLC or TLC. Thus it is unlikely that the abuse of etorphine could be detected by commonly used urine screening methods.'" Masters put the paper down and looked across at Watling. "So you see, Doctor, the fact that all your tests failed to show etorphine is, in itself, a positive result. And far from being unhelpful, your work has been of great value."

"Thank heaven for that. There is just one snag."

"What's that?"

"What if the defence can produce information that there is some other obscure drug, somewhere in the world, that is equally undetectable by those methods. We have no case unless we can say etorphine is unique."

"Again a very good point," said Masters. "But there is very little we can do about that except to point out that any obscure drug they dredge up was unlikely to have been available to kill those two men, whereas the etorphine was known to be at hand. Circumstantial, no doubt, but circumstantial evidence is often very powerful in court, as we all know."

Watling nodded, and held out his hand. "May I see those papers, Mr Masters. For my own satisfaction, that is. It seems that in Lincoln we're a little behind in our current knowledge."

Masters handed them over. "Keep them, Doctor. I'll get more photocopies from the RSM."

"Thanks."

"Now what?" asked Green.

"I've talked enough for the moment," said Masters. "You carry on, please."

"Fair enough," replied Green. "You've heard about the means used for killing Belton and Heberden. The motive, which we don't have to show, but which helps in court, was Happy's certainty that Melada had been killed by Belton. You've heard how she came to that conclusion and, indeed, how she proved it to her own satisfaction. We shall contend that revenge for Melada's death caused her to plan Belton's murder and then Heberden's. We have not questioned her on these points yet, but we believe that though she had asked Belton to help her to stop Melada buying the church, she did not want her man stopped quite as finally as he was. We think that the shock of Melada's death and her intention to revenge herself on Belton caused her to regard Heberden, who was an unwitting partner to the cause of the tragedy, as equally guilty with or as an accomplice of Belton. To a mind sufficiently deranged to plan a murder, the fact that Heberden had put up five thousand quid to help do Melada down was sufficient to brand him as second murderer. Have I made myself clear, so far?"

Everybody present agreed Green had made his point.

"Good. Now carrying on from there, we reckon that Happy, being a clever little thing, had to think of where to dispose of Belton's body. Now we don't know whether she guessed Melada's body was in the vicinity of the church or not, but we do know that on the first occasion on which she visited St John's she was left alone in the churchyard for some considerable time while Melada went with the vicar to collect the key. We also know that she looked round the churchyard and while doing that she couldn't fail to see the well, just as we did when we went there first. So, wondering where to hide the body, she thinks of the well."

"That's all very well," said Webb, "but how did she get Belton to go there?"

"We'll have to see what she says about that, but I reckon if you'd buried the body of a man you'd killed in a church-yard, and that man's wife rings up and says: 'Will you meet me at the church, there's something I want to say to you or show you?' What would be your reaction? You're not to know she's chosen that place because it's got a well in which to hide your body. You think she's discovered something else—something you'd rather not have uncovered."

"Melada's body?"

"Of course. The one thing uppermost in your mind is that body, so when somebody asks you to meet them where you've buried it, you're bound to fear the worst. Certainly you can't refuse to go. You've got to go. Just in case there's something that's given you away."

"Even, I suppose," said Berger, "you might have to be prepared to kill again."

"Right, lad. Belton may have thought he'd have to si-lence Happy. But when he arrives, she asks him to look at the well because there's something funny about it. Full of relief that she hasn't found the grave, he's a bit off guard, and goes to the well. She's close by and does her stuff with her etorphine needle or bit of twig or whatever she used. He doesn't know what's hit him. In no time at all he's dead, and all she has to do is tumble him down the shaft. He's walked there on his own two feet, remember, and so she just pulls or nudges him over until gravity and his own weight do the rest. Exit Belton.

"She's gone to the church on her Chopper bike. Now she puts this in the back of the car and drives to Lincoln. She takes the Chopper out in some quiet place where she can leave it, handy, and drives the car to a spot where it is certain to cause an immediate obstruction in the road and so gets towed away by the police. She gets out, locks the car, and walks back to the Chopper. She may even have gone to her house, The Shack, to offload the Chopper and gone back by bus after leaving the car."

"It all sounds right," said Watling. "If it is, the SCO should be able to support your theory with dust samples, fingerprints and so on."

"But," said Reed, "there's a snag when it comes to Heberden, isn't there?"

"In what way?"

"It took two of us dirty great coppers to lift him out of that tomb. How would a slip of a girl get him in?"

"Easy, laddie," said Green. "We'll prove it this afternoon, using a policewoman. But being small for that job is an advantage. Young Happy could line up the body end on to the tomb, then she could literally get through those arches and stand in the hole itself. Then all she had to do was get hold of the ankles and heave. A body as thin as Heberden's would go through the end arch easily enough. She'd have him half in in no time. The only difficult bit would be the last pull to get him right in. But there again, where you couldn't easily get your shoulders through the arch, she could. And once she gave the last heave ... well, his shoulders and head would fall in, wouldn't they?"

"I suppose you're going to tell us she phoned Heberden and got him to the church on some pretext?"

"That's right. She repeated her method. What would be easier than to tell Heberden she'd lost a bit of jewelry in the church? Would he mind bringing the key so that she could look for it? A gentlemanly old boy like Heberden would agree like a shot if a woman's in distress. He was probably on his hands and knees near the altar helping her look for her ring when she administered the etorphine. Knowing the way Happy planned this, I'd gamble she got him to die within feet of where she wanted him."

"She sounds a fiend incarnate," said Watling.

"You'd think she was quite a sweet lass, actually."

"Would I?"

182

"I reckon so. We all did. And now, to finish up. I personally found the ironmonger who remembers serving a young lady with glasses with a hell of a lot of resin glue."

"You did?" asked Berger. "When?"

"Yesterday, son, while you were busy with other chores. Somebody had to do something positive."

"Has she been identified?"

"Not yet, lad, but she will be, tomorrow."

Almost twenty-four hours later, Masters and Green were with Webb in the local man's office.

"She's denying everything," said Green.

"Did you expect her to confess?" asked Webb.

"Not really. She's holding out because she doesn't know how much we've got."

"The ironmonger's positive identification, the wheel-prints of her Chopper in both cars; no fingerprints because she wiped them off; and only a possibility that the SCO can prove any sort of dust transference."

"The sergeants are still searching the house, remember. They may find something."

"Agreed," said Webb, "but I wish Watling had been able to prove the etorphine theory. It would have made it so much more solid."

There was a knock at the door.

"Come in."

The station sergeant put his head round the door. "Dr Watling to see Superintendent Masters, sir."

"Talk of the devil. Show him in, please."

Watling came in looking well pleased with himself. "Morning, gentlemen."

"Good morning, Doctor. We weren't expecting to see you, but it's a pleasant surprise."

"It's almost time for a drink. Will you join us at The Chestnut Tree."

"I'm always willing to take a drink off anybody. Can I talk as we go?"

"Come on." As they reached the pavement Watling said,

"Those papers, Mr Masters. Wonderful. I studied them very carefully after you left me yesterday."

"And?"

"One paragraph interested me greatly. You may remember the bit I'm referring to. The one which starts by saying there are no human metabolic studies of etorphine."

"I remember. I recall thinking that if there are no metabolic reports I couldn't very well blame you for producing a nil return."

"Nice of you. But later on it goes on to say that the TLC analyses were first performed after acid hydrolysis of the urine since this is the most commonly used method. And that's what I did. But those researchers did a sort of control test with uncontaminated urine. They added etorphine to the urine after hydrolysis and got a result. Then they added it to uncontaminated urine before hydrolysis, and the result was barely discernible. So they came to the conclusion that the severe conditions of the acid hydrolysis procedure destroy about ninety-five percent of the etorphine."

They had reached The Chestnut Tree. As they went in at the door, Green said: "And ninety-five per cent of nothing leaves you with nothing to work on, doc?"

"Exactly. But they went on to say that the gentle procedure of glucuronidase hydrolysis was found not to alter the sensitivity of detection by TLC."

"So what have you done, doctor?"

"Repeated the TLC analyses."

"And?"

"Bingo. A trace! A spot! Nothing more! But enough. My colleague and I can both go into the witness box and state on oath that we have found traces of etorphine in both bodies."

Masters smiled happily. "That, Dr Watling, earns you the double of your choice."

"I thought it might. Malt whiskey, please."

It was while they were sitting round the table in the

bar that Reed and Berger arrived.

"Anything?" asked Green.

"What would you like?" asked Reed.

"Mine's a pint."

"In the way of evidence?"

Masters got to his feet. "Don't tell me she failed to throw away the keys of those two cars?"

Reed stared after him, open-mouthed, as he went to the bar to order drinks for the newcomers.

"How the hell did he know that?" asked Berger, as though unable to believe what he had heard.

"He's jammy," retorted Green. "Jammy. I've always said so, and you two should know that by now."

Masters came back carrying two pints.

"The key to the church wasn't with them by any chance?"

Slowly Reed drew two envelopes out of his pocket and put them on the table. They both sounded as though they contained hard, metallic objects.

THE PERENNIAL LIBRARY MYSTERY SERIES

Ted Allbeury

THE OTHER SIDE OF SILENCE   P 669, $2.84
"In the best le Carré tradition . . . an ingenious and readable book."
  —*New York Times Book Review*

PALOMINO BLONDE   P 670, $2.84
"Fast-moving, splendidly technocratic intercontinental espionage tale
. . . you'll love it."   —*The Times* (London)

SNOWBALL   P 671, $2.84
"A novel of byzantine intrigue. . . ."—*New York Times Book Review*

Delano Ames

CORPSE DIPLOMATIQUE   P 637, $2.84
"Sprightly and intelligent."
  —*New York Herald Tribune Book Review*

FOR OLD CRIME'S SAKE   P 629, $2.84

MURDER, MAESTRO, PLEASE   P 630, $2.84
"If there is a more engaging couple in modern fiction than Jane and
Dagobert Brown, we have not met them."   —*Scotsman*

SHE SHALL HAVE MURDER   P 638, $2.84
"Combines the merit of both the English and American schools in the
new mystery. It's as breezy as the best of the American ones, and has
the sophistication and wit of any top-notch Britisher."
  —*New York Herald Tribune Book Review*

E. C. Bentley

TRENT'S LAST CASE   P 440, $2.50
"One of the three best detective stories ever written."
  —Agatha Christie

TRENT'S OWN CASE   P 516, $2.25
"I won't waste time saying that the plot is sound and the detection
satisfying. Trent has not altered a scrap and reappears with all his old
humor and charm."   —Dorothy L. Sayers

Andrew Bergman

THE BIG KISS-OFF OF 1944   P 673, $2.84
"It is without doubt the nearest thing to genuine Chandler I've ever come across. . . . Tough, witty—very witty—and a beautiful eye for period detail. . . ."   —Jack Higgins

HOLLYWOOD AND LEVINE   P 674, $2.84
"Fast-paced private-eye fiction."   —San Francisco Chronicle

Gavin Black

A DRAGON FOR CHRISTMAS   P 473, $1.95
"Potent excitement!"   —New York Herald Tribune

THE EYES AROUND ME   P 485, $1.95
"I stayed up until all hours last night reading *The Eyes Around Me,* which is something I do not do very often, but I was so intrigued by the ingeniousness of Mr. Black's plotting and the witty way in which he spins his mystery. I can only say that I enjoyed the book enormously."
                                            —F. van Wyck Mason

YOU WANT TO DIE, JOHNNY?   P 472, $1.95
"Gavin Black doesn't just develop a pressure plot in suspense, he adds uninfected wit, character, charm, and sharp knowledge of the Far East to make rereading as keen as the first race-through."   —Book Week

Nicholas Blake

THE CORPSE IN THE SNOWMAN   P 427, $1.95
"If there is a distinction between the novel and the detective story (which we do not admit), then this book deserves a high place in both categories."   —New York Times

END OF CHAPTER   P 397, $1.95
". . . admirably solid . . . an adroit formal detective puzzle backed up by firm characterization and a knowing picture of London publishing."
                                            —New York Times

HEAD OF A TRAVELER   P 398, $2.25
"Another grade A detective story of the right old jigsaw persuasion."
                               —New York Herald Tribune Book Review

MINUTE FOR MURDER   P 419, $1.95
"An outstanding mystery novel. Mr. Blake's writing is a delight in itself."   —New York Times

THE MORNING AFTER DEATH   P 520, $1.95
"One of Blake's best."   —Rex Warner

A PENKNIFE IN MY HEART   P 521, $2.25
"Style brilliant . . . and suspenseful."   —*San Francisco Chronicle*

THE PRIVATE WOUND   P 531, $2.25
"[Blake's] best novel in a dozen years . . . . An intensely penetrating study of sexual passion. . . . A powerful story of murder and its aftermath."
                                    —Anthony Boucher, *New York Times*

A QUESTION OF PROOF   P 494, $1.95
"The characters in this story are unusually well drawn, and the suspense is well sustained."   —*New York Times*

THE SAD VARIETY   P 495, $2.25
"It is a stunner. I read it instead of eating, instead of sleeping."
                                    —Dorothy Salisbury Davis

THERE'S TROUBLE BREWING   P 569, $3.37
"Nigel Strangeways is a puzzling mixture of simplicity and penetration, but all the more real for that."
                          —*The Times* (London) *Literary Supplement*

THOU SHELL OF DEATH   P 428, $1.95
"It has all the virtues of culture, intelligence and sensibility that the most exacting connoisseur could ask of detective fiction."
                          —*The Times* (London) *Literary Supplement*

THE WIDOW'S CRUISE   P 399, $2.25
"A stirring suspense. . . . The thrilling tale leaves nothing to be desired."
                                    —*Springfield Republican*

Oliver Bleeck

THE BRASS GO-BETWEEN   P 645, $2.84
"Fiction with a flair, well above the norm for thrillers."
                                    —*Associated Press*

THE PROCANE CHRONICLE   P 647, $2.84
"Without peer in American suspense."   —*Los Angeles Times*

PROTOCOL FOR A KIDNAPPING   P 646, $2.84
"The zigzags of plot are electric; the characters sharp; but it is the wit and irony and touches of plain fun which make the whole a standout."
                                    —*Los Angeles Times*

John & Emery Bonett

A BANNER FOR PEGASUS   P 554, $2.40
"A gem! Beautifully plotted and set. . . . Not only is the murder adroit
and deserved, and the detection competent, but the love story is charming."   —Jacques Barzun and Wendell Hertig Taylor

DEAD LION   P 563, $2.40
"A clever plot, authentic background and interesting characters highly
recommended this one."   —*New Republic*

THE SOUND OF MURDER   P 642, $2.84
The suspects are many, the clues few, but the gentle Inspector ferrets out
the truth and pursues the case to its bitter and shocking end.

Christianna Brand

GREEN FOR DANGER   P 551, $2.50
"You have to reach for the greatest of Great Names (Christie, Carr,
Queen . . .) to find Brand's rivals in the devious subtleties of the trade."
                        —Anthony Boucher

TOUR DE FORCE   P 572, $2.40
"Complete with traps for the over-ingenious, a double-reverse surprise
ending and a key clue planted so fairly and obviously that you completely
overlook it. If that's your idea of perfect entertainment, then seize at once
upon *Tour de Force.*"   —Anthony Boucher, *New York Times*

James Byrom

OR BE HE DEAD   P 585, $2.84
"A very original tale . . . Well written and steadily entertaining."
  —Jacques Barzun and Wendell Hertig Taylor, *A Catalogue of Crime*

Henry Calvin

IT'S DIFFERENT ABROAD   P 640, $2.84
"What is remarkable and delightful, Mr. Calvin imparts a flavor of satire
to what he renovates and compels us to take straight."
                        —Jacques Barzun

Marjorie Carleton

VANISHED   P 559, $2.40
"Exceptional . . . a minor triumph."
  —Jacques Barzun and Wendell Hertig Taylor, *A Catalogue of Crime*

George Harmon Coxe

MURDER WITH PICTURES   P 527, $2.25

"[Coxe] has hit the bull's-eye with his first shot."

—*New York Times*

Edmund Crispin

BURIED FOR PLEASURE   P 506, $2.50

"Absolute and unalloyed delight."

—Anthony Boucher, *New York Times*

Lionel Davidson

THE MENORAH MEN   P 592, $2.84

"Of his fellow thriller writers, only John Le Carré shows the same instinct for the viscera."   —*Chicago Tribune*

NIGHT OF WENCESLAS   P 595, $2.84

"A most ingenious thriller, so enriched with style, wit, and a sense of serious comedy that it all but transcends its kind."

—*The New Yorker*

THE ROSE OF TIBET   P 593, $2.84

"I hadn't realized how much I missed the genuine Adventure story . . . until I read *The Rose of Tibet*."   —Graham Greene

D. M. Devine

MY BROTHER'S KILLER   P 558, $2.40

"A most enjoyable crime story which I enjoyed reading down to the last moment."   —Agatha Christie

Kenneth Fearing

THE BIG CLOCK   P 500, $1.95

"It will be some time before chill-hungry clients meet again so rare a compound of irony, satire, and icy-fingered narrative. *The Big Clock* is . . . a psychothriller you won't put down."   —*Weekly Book Review*

Andrew Garve

THE ASHES OF LODA   P 430, $1.50

"Garve . . . embellishes a fine fast adventure story with a more credible picture of the U.S.S.R. than is offered in most thrillers."

—*New York Times Book Review*

THE CUCKOO LINE AFFAIR   P 451, $1.95

". . . an agreeable and ingenious piece of work."   —*The New Yorker*

A HERO FOR LEANDA P 429, $1.50

"One can trust Mr. Garve to put a fresh twist to any situation, and the ending is really a lovely surprise." —*Manchester Guardian*

MURDER THROUGH THE LOOKING GLASS P 449, $1.95

". . . refreshingly out-of-the-way and enjoyable . . . highly recommended to all comers." —*Saturday Review*

NO TEARS FOR HILDA P 441, $1.95

"It starts fine and finishes finer. I got behind on breathing watching Max get not only his man but his woman, too." —*Rex Stout*

THE RIDDLE OF SAMSON P 450, $1.95

"The story is an excellent one, the people are quite likable, and the writing is superior." —*Springfield Republican*

Michael Gilbert

BLOOD AND JUDGMENT P 446, $1.95

"Gilbert readers need scarcely be told that the characters all come alive at first sight, and that his surpassing talent for narration enhances any plot. . . . Don't miss." —*San Francisco Chronicle*

THE BODY OF A GIRL P 459, $1.95

"Does what a good mystery should do: open up into all kinds of ramifications, with untold menace behind the action. At the end, there is a bang-up climax, and it is a pleasure to see how skilfully Gilbert wraps everything up." —*New York Times Book Review*

FEAR TO TREAD P 458, $1.95

"Merits serious consideration as a work of art." —*New York Times*

Joe Gores

HAMMETT P 631, $2.84

"Joe Gores at his very best. Terse, powerful writing—with the master, Dashiell Hammett, as the protagonist in a novel I think he would have been proud to call his own." —*Robert Ludlum*

C. W. Grafton

BEYOND A REASONABLE DOUBT P 519, $1.95

"A very ingenious tale of murder . . . a brilliant and gripping narrative." —*Jacques Barzun and Wendell Hertig Taylor*

C. W. Grafton (cont'd)

THE RAT BEGAN TO GNAW THE ROPE P 639, $2.84
"Fast, humorous story with flashes of brilliance."

—*The New Yorker*

Edward Grierson

THE SECOND MAN P 528, $2.25
"One of the best trial-testimony books to have come along in quite a while." —*The New Yorker*

Bruce Hamilton

TOO MUCH OF WATER P 635, $2.84
"A superb sea mystery. . . . The prose is excellent."
—Jacques Barzun and Wendell Hertig Taylor, *A Catalogue of Crime*

Cyril Hare

DEATH IS NO SPORTSMAN P 555, $2.40
"You will be thrilled because it succeeds in placing an ingenious story in a new and refreshing setting. . . . The identity of the murderer is really a surprise." —*Daily Mirror*

DEATH WALKS THE WOODS P 556, $2.40
"Here is a fine formal detective story, with a technically brilliant solution demanding the attention of all connoisseurs of construction."
—Anthony Boucher, *New York Times Book Review*

AN ENGLISH MURDER P 455, $2.50
"By a long shot, the best crime story I have read for a long time. Everything is traditional, but originality does not suffer. The setting is perfect. Full marks to Mr. Hare." —*Irish Press*

SUICIDE EXCEPTED P 636, $2.84
"Adroit in its manipulation . . . and distinguished by a plot-twister which I'll wager Christie wishes she'd thought of." —*New York Times*

TENANT FOR DEATH P 570, $2.84
"The way in which an air of probability is combined both with clear, terse narrative and with a good deal of subtle suburban atmosphere, proves the extreme skill of the writer." —*The Spectator*

TRAGEDY AT LAW P 522, $2.25
"An extremely urbane and well-written detective story."

—*New York Times*

UNTIMELY DEATH   P 514, $2.25
"The English detective story at its quiet best, meticulously underplayed, rich in perceivings of the droll human animal and ready at the last with a neat surprise which has been there all the while had we but wits to see it."   —*New York Herald Tribune Book Review*

THE WIND BLOWS DEATH   P 589, $2.84
"A plot compounded of musical knowledge, a Dickens allusion, and a subtle point in law is related with delightfully unobtrusive wit, warmth, and style."   —*New York Times*

WITH A BARE BODKIN   P 523, $2.25
"One of the best detective stories published for a long time."
                                                   —*The Spectator*

Robert Harling

THE ENORMOUS SHADOW   P 545, $2.50
"In some ways the best spy story of the modern period. . . . The writing is terse and vivid . . . the ending full of action . . . altogether first-rate."
—Jacques Barzun and Wendell Hertig Taylor, *A Catalogue of Crime*

Matthew Head

THE CABINDA AFFAIR   P 541, $2.25
"An absorbing whodunit and a distinguished novel of atmosphere."
                          —Anthony Boucher, *New York Times*

THE CONGO VENUS   P 597, $2.84
"Terrific. The dialogue is just plain wonderful."   —*Boston Globe*

MURDER AT THE FLEA CLUB   P 542, $2.50
"The true delight is in Head's style, its limpid ease combined with humor and an awesome precision of phrase."   —*San Francisco Chronicle*

M. V. Heberden

ENGAGED TO MURDER   P 533, $2.25
"Smooth plotting."   —*New York Times*

James Hilton

WAS IT MURDER?   P 501, $1.95
"The story is well planned and well written."   —*New York Times*

S. B. Hough

DEAR DAUGHTER DEAD   P 661, $2.84
"A highly intelligent and sophisticated story of police detection . . . not
to be missed on any account."   —Francis Iles, *The Guardian*

SWEET SISTER SEDUCED   P 662, $2.84
In the course of a nightlong conversation between the Inspector and the
suspect, the complex emotions of a very strange marriage are revealed.

P. M. Hubbard

HIGH TIDE   P 571, $2.40
"A smooth elaboration of mounting horror and danger."

                                                —*Library Journal*

Elspeth Huxley

THE AFRICAN POISON MURDERS   P 540, $2.25
"Obscure venom, manical mutilations, deadly bush fire, thrilling climax
compose major opus.... Top-flight."

                                —*Saturday Review of Literature*

MURDER ON SAFARI   P 587, $2.84
"Right now we'd call Mrs. Huxley a dangerous rival to Agatha Christie."   —*Books*

Francis Iles

BEFORE THE FACT   P 517, $2.50
"Not many 'serious' novelists have produced character studies to compare with Iles's internally terrifying portrait of the murderer in *Before
the Fact,* his masterpiece and a work truly deserving the appellation of
unique and beyond price."   —Howard Haycraft

MALICE AFORETHOUGHT   P 532, $1.95
"It is a long time since I have read anything so good as *Malice Aforethought,* with its cynical humour, acute criminology, plausible detail and
rapid movement. It makes you hug yourself with pleasure."

                                —H. C. Harwood, *Saturday Review*

Michael Innes

APPLEBY ON ARARAT   P 648, $2.84
"Superbly plotted and humorously written."   —*The New Yorker*

APPLEBY'S END   P 649, $2.84
"Most amusing."   —*Boston Globe*

THE CASE OF THE JOURNEYING BOY P 632, $3.12
"I could see no faults in it. There is no one to compare with him."
     —Illustrated London News

DEATH ON A QUIET DAY P 677, $2.84
"Delightfully witty."   *—Chicago Sunday Tribune*

DEATH BY WATER P 574, $2.40
"The amount of ironic social criticism and deft characterization of scenes
and people would serve another author for six books."
    —Jacques Barzun and Wendell Hertig Taylor

HARE SITTING UP P 590, $2.84
"There is hardly anyone (in mysteries or mainstream) more exquisitely
literate, allusive and Jamesian—and hardly anyone with a firmer sense
of melodramatic plot or a more vigorous gift of storytelling."
    —Anthony Boucher, New York Times

THE LONG FAREWELL P 575, $2.40
"A model of the deft, classic detective story, told in the most wittily
diverting prose."   *—New York Times*

THE MAN FROM THE SEA P 591, $2.84
"The pace is brisk, the adventures exciting and excitingly told, and above
all he keeps to the very end the interesting ambiguity of the man from
the sea."   *—New Statesman*

ONE MAN SHOW P 672, $2.84
"Exciting, amusingly written . . . very good enjoyment it is."
    —The Spectator

THE SECRET VANGUARD P 584, $2.84
"Innes . . . has mastered the art of swift, exciting and well-organized
narrative."   *—New York Times*

THE WEIGHT OF THE EVIDENCE P 633, $2.84
"First-class puzzle, deftly solved. University background interesting and
amusing."   *—Saturday Review of Literature*

Mary Kelly

THE SPOILT KILL P 565, $2.40
"Mary Kelly is a new Dorothy Sayers. . . . [An] exciting new novel."
    —Evening News

Lange Lewis

THE BIRTHDAY MURDER   P 518, $1.95

"Almost perfect in its playlike purity and delightful prose."
—Jacques Barzun and Wendell Hertig Taylor

Allan MacKinnon

HOUSE OF DARKNESS   P 582, $2.84

"His best . . . a perfect compendium."
—Jacques Barzun and Wendell Hertig Taylor, *A Catalogue of Crime*

Frank Parrish

FIRE IN THE BARLEY   P 651, $2.84

"A remarkable and brilliant first novel. . . . entrancing."
—*The Spectator*

SNARE IN THE DARK   P 650, $2.84

The wily English poacher Dan Mallett is framed for murder and has to confront unknown enemies to clear himself.

STING OF THE HONEYBEE   P 652, $2.84

"Terrorism and murder visit a sleepy English village in this witty, offbeat thriller."   —*Chicago Sun-Times*

Austin Ripley

MINUTE MYSTERIES   P 387, $2.50

More than one hundred of the world's shortest detective stories. Only one possible solution to each case!

Thomas Sterling

THE EVIL OF THE DAY   P 529, $2.50

"Prose as witty and subtle as it is sharp and clear. . .characters unconventionally conceived and richly bodied forth . . . . In short, a novel to be treasured."   —Anthony Boucher, *New York Times*

Julian Symons

THE BELTING INHERITANCE   P 468, $1.95

"A superb whodunit in the best tradition of the detective story."
—August Derleth, *Madison Capital Times*

BOGUE'S FORTUNE   P 481, $1.95

"There's a touch of the old sardonic humour, and more than a touch of style."   —*The Spectator*

Julian Symons (cont'd)

THE COLOR OF MURDER P 461, $1.95

"A singularly unostentatious and memorably brilliant detective story."
— *New York Herald Tribune Book Review*

Dorothy Stockbridge Tillet
(John Stephen Strange)

THE MAN WHO KILLED FORTESCUE P 536, $2.25

"Better than average." — *Saturday Review of Literature*

Simon Troy

THE ROAD TO RHUINE P 583, $2.84

"Unusual and agreeably told." — *San Francisco Chronicle*

SWIFT TO ITS CLOSE P 546, $2.40

"A nicely literate British mystery . . . the atmosphere and the plot are exceptionally well wrought, the dialogue excellent." — *Best Sellers*

Henry Wade

THE DUKE OF YORK'S STEPS P 588, $2.84

"A classic of the golden age."
— Jacques Barzun and Wendell Hertig Taylor, *A Catalogue of Crime*

A DYING FALL P 543, $2.50

"One of those expert British suspense jobs . . . it crackles with undercurrents of blackmail, violent passion and murder. Topnotch in its class."
— *Time*

THE HANGING CAPTAIN P 548, $2.50

"This is a detective story for connoisseurs, for those who value clear thinking and good writing above mere ingenuity and easy thrills."
— *The Times* (London) *Literary Supplement*

Hillary Waugh

LAST SEEN WEARING . . . P 552, $2.40

"A brilliant tour de force." — Julian Symons

THE MISSING MAN P 553, $2.40

"The quiet detailed police work of Chief Fred C. Fellows, Stockford, Conn., is at its best in *The Missing Man* . . . one of the Chief's toughest cases and one of the best handled."
— Anthony Boucher, *New York Times Book Review*

Henry Kitchell Webster

WHO IS THE NEXT?   P 539, $2.25
"A double murder, private-plane piloting, a neat impersonation, and a delicate courtship are adroitly combined by a writer who knows how to use the language."   —Jacques Barzun and Wendell Hertig Taylor

John Welcome

GO FOR BROKE   P 663, $2.84
A rich financier chases Richard Graham half 'round Europe in a desperate attempt to prevent the truth getting out.

RUN FOR COVER   P 664, $2.84
"I can think of few writers in the international intrigue game with such a gift for fast and vivid storytelling."
                    —*New York Times Book Review*

STOP AT NOTHING   P 665, $2.84
"Mr. Welcome is lively, vivid and highly readable."
                    —*New York Times Book Review*

Anna Mary Wells

MURDERER'S CHOICE   P 534, $2.50
"Good writing, ample action, and excellent character work."
                    —*Saturday Review of Literature*

A TALENT FOR MURDER   P 535, $2.25
"The discovery of the villain is a decided shock."   —*Books*

Charles Williams

DEAD CALM   P 655, $2.84
"A brilliant tour de force of inventive plotting, fine manipulation of a small cast and breathtaking sequences of spectacular navigation."
                    —*New York Times Book Review*

THE SAILCLOTH SHROUD   P 654, $2.84
"A fine novel of excitement, spirited, fresh and satisfying."
                    —*New York Times*

THE WRONG VENUS   P 656, $2.84
Swindler Lawrence Colby and the lovely Martine create a story of romance, larceny, and very blunt homicide.

Edward Young

THE FIFTH PASSENGER   P 544, $2.25
"Clever and adroit . . . excellent thriller. . . ."   —*Library Journal*

If you enjoyed this book you'll want to know about
THE PERENNIAL LIBRARY MYSTERY SERIES

Buy them at your local bookstore or use this coupon for ordering:

Qty	P number	Price

	postage and handling charge	$1.00
	_____ book(s) @ $0.25	
	TOTAL	

Prices contained in this coupon are Harper & Row invoice prices only. They are subject to change without notice, and in no way reflect the prices at which these books may be sold by other suppliers.

HARPER & ROW, Mail Order Dept. #PMS, 10 East 53rd St., New York, N.Y. 10022.

Please send me the books I have checked above. I am enclosing $_____ which includes a postage and handling charge of $1.00 for the first book and 25¢ for each additional book. Send check or money order. No cash or C.O.D.s please

Name_____

Address_____

City_____ State_____ Zip_____

Please allow 4 weeks for delivery. USA only. This offer expires 1/31/86
Please add applicable sales tax.